Olivia and the Little Way

Nancy Carabio Belanger

Harv
Pub

ISBN: 978-0-923568-92-4

To order additional copies, please contact:
Harvey House Publishing
P.O. Box 81841
Rochester, MI 48308
www.littleflowerbook.com

Selected quotations excerpted from:

Saint Thérèse of Lisieux, The Story of a Soul. TAN Books and Publishers, Inc., 1997. Rockford, IL.

Society of the Little Flower. Darien, IL. www.littleflower.org

Letters of St. Thérèse of Lisieux Volume 1 1877-1890. Translated by John Clarke, O.C.D. Copyright 1982 by Washington Province of Discalced Carmelites, Inc. ICS Publications, Washington, D.C.

Letters of St. Thérèse of Lisieux Volume 2 1890-1897. Translated by John Clarke, O.C.D. Copyright 1988 by Washington Province of Discalced Carmelites, Inc. ICS Publications, Washington, D.C.

Printed in the United States of America

"Anyone who has discovered Christ must lead others to Him. A great joy cannot be kept to oneself. It has to be passed on."
—Pope Benedict XVI

"Jesus, I want to tell all little souls of the wonder of your love."
—St. Thérèse of Lisieux

"I will raise up a mighty host of little saints. My mission is to make God loved...."
—St. Thérèse of Lisieux

"This book offers a unique and fresh way to celebrate the life of St. Thérèse of Lisieux. It is a wonderful and engaging novel suitable for all but especially for 'tweens. They can share Olivia's life lessons as she deals with different relationships and real challenges."

—Catholic Press Association

"This endearing story gave me a new appreciation for St. Thérèse's spirituality and how it can be applied in our everyday lives. *Olivia and the Little Way* made this year's celebration of St. Thérèse's feast day much more meaningful for me."

—Sr. Barbara Berg, SHSp
Director of Religious Education, Basilica of the National Shrine of the Little Flower, San Antonio, TX

"I found myself cheering for Olivia as she struggles with new friends and a new school. I enjoyed the marvelous weaving of St. Thérèse's life and quotes into Olivia's own life. It is a delight to read such a Catholic book that is uplifting and entertaining without being too 'preachy.' Olivia could be you (or me) with messy room and all.

"Olivia was such a normal girl with real problems that so many of us face—even if we aren't in 5th grade anymore! Making good choices, struggling with tough decisions. We can often feel alone in our struggles but Olivia discovers as we all must do that we are never alone. God is there and together with great saints, such as the Little Flower, we can discover that we can do more than we think we can."

—Rachel Watkins
Developer/Creator of the Little Flowers Girls Club • www.eccehomopress.com

Special thanks to all of my friends who have prayed for and encouraged me during the writing of this book, especially Anne, Katie, Tracey, Kelly, Amy, Liza, Jenny, Julie, and Mary Pat, the best of friends who patiently listened to me spout out all of my ideas and concerns over coffee and bagels. Thanks for telling me I could do it.

To my grandparents in Heaven, who taught me about love and family.

To Erin and Bardz at DDM Publications: I owe you a lot of Tex-Mex!

Special thanks to Sandra Casali LewAllen, who supported this idea with gusto and gave the illustrations such beauty and grace.

To Mom and Dad, and Joe(y), for always loving me and making me laugh so hard it hurts.

To the entire Belanger family for their love and support.

To Lauren and Anna: I hope you enjoy this story. Hugs and kisses!

To Vincent and Paul, gifts from God. Thank you for helping me with ideas for this story. I love you to the ends of the earth and back!

To John-Paul, my patient and helpful husband. I love you!

To St. Thérèse, my dear sister in Heaven: This is for you.

And, of course, to God, who is love. He makes all things possible.

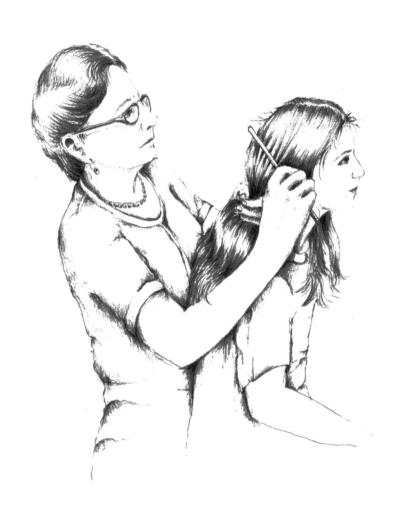

One

"I rejoice to be little, because only children and those who are like them will be admitted to the heavenly banquet."
—St. Thérèse

The midsummer sun warmed Olivia's face as Grandma Rosemary brushed her hair in long strokes. It sure felt good to have someone brush your hair, especially your grandma.

Olivia was closer to her Grandma Rosemary than to anyone else in the world. Olivia had a handful of friends back home in Texas, but when she spent a good part of July every year with Grandma in Michigan, it was heaven, just the two of them. It became a summer tradition two years ago when Grandpa died. Mom and Dad thought it would be a great cure for Grandma's loneliness to have Olivia spend some time with her over the summer break.

They always had such fun together playing solitaire with the deck of cards Grandma and Grandpa had gotten from a famous hotel on Mackinac Island. They'd play out on the screened-in back porch, which was framed with rose bushes Grandpa had planted many summers ago, before Olivia was even born, or her parents were even married. Grandma tended those roses like you would a child, caring for them and nurturing them each season.

That part of the house faced the south, where the rosebushes could get sunshine all day long. Her favorites were tea roses, whose tiny pink buds bloomed every summer, awash with a delicate but beautiful fragrance Olivia loved. Grandma would tell Olivia their fancy-sounding names, like Serendipity, an apricot-pink rose, and Earth Song, Olivia's favorite pink variety.

They would spend the day at the park on nice days, or the library if it rained, and Grandma would take Olivia to McDonald's for French fries as a treat.

In the evenings they would watch *Wheel of Fortune* on Grandma's flowered sofa, while they each ate a simple supper off of TV trays. Olivia would try to guess the phrases, but never got any of them. Grandma Rosemary used to solve them all of the time.

She would tell the contestants to buy vowels, as if they could hear her.

"Buy an E!" she would urge a contestant on the TV, so excited was she to solve the puzzle.

Often Grandma would wake Olivia up early so they could walk to morning Mass at Our Lady of Good Counsel, an old church on Grandma's street. It was a lot different from Olivia's more modern-looking church in Texas. Here at Grandma's church there were more statues and pretty stained-glass windows that burst into color when the morning sunshine streamed through them.

After Mass they would go over to light a candle in front of a statue of a pretty saint who held a bouquet of roses. Grandma would drop some coins into the metal box and take a long match to light a candle in a red votive. She would make the sign of the cross and fold her hands in prayer, silently moving her lips with her eyes closed. Then Grandma would open her eyes, make the sign of the cross again, take Olivia's hand, and together they would walk back home and eat fresh cantaloupe or strawberries for a snack before deciding what to do for the day.

Grandma Rosemary and Olivia would talk about everything and share secrets and tales from Grandma's past. She'd tell stories about how Grandpa used to work for Ford Motor Company and how he loved to garden. Grandma would tell tales of her life as a young woman before she got married, how she was a seamstress in a fine clothing shop for ladies. Olivia loved hearing her grandmother tell her stories of the rich ladies who would come in needing work on their fancy ball gowns for big parties. She liked to pretend she was one of them in front of Grandma's full-length mirror. She'd put on one of her sundresses with Grandma's big plastic costume jewelry and twirl around, admiring herself in the mirror. Sometimes Grandma would even let her add a small dab of her lipstick as she pretended she was one of the ladies in the dress shop.

"So, just think—in one month you'll be moving here to Michigan. How do you feel about that?" Grandma asked as she brushed Olivia's long brown hair.

Olivia closed her eyes against the sunshine and leaned back in the lawn chair in the back yard.

"It's okay, I guess," she said. "I'm glad I'll be close by you though. That's the only part that's good."

Grandma began to part Olivia's hair down the middle to start a French braid.

"But you'll miss Texas?" she asked.

"Mmm hmm. And Claire and Emily." Those were Olivia's two best friends. She was worried they'd forget about her when she moved, even though they had promised to write letters. "I sure hope I fit in at this new school."

"Your daddy's job is important, and the company wants him to move here. I admit I am glad you and Baby Lucy and your mom and dad are moving, Sweetie. I've missed you so much, especially after Grandpa died." Grandma's voice got soft and sounded far away.

"I know, Grandma. I guess I'm just a little nervous." Olivia bit her lip. She felt sad when they talked about Grandpa. She knew he was in Heaven with Jesus and all of the saints, but it was hard not having him in the little house with Grandma. Sometimes it felt like he wasn't really gone at all, just in the basement tinkering around in his workshop and would soon be upstairs in the kitchen making tuna fish sandwiches for everyone. The smell of tuna fish still reminded Olivia of Grandpa.

"You're going to like St. Michael's School, Livvy. You know my friend Mrs. Stewart? Her granddaughter Hayley goes there and is in fifth grade, too. I'll introduce you so you will know someone. Won't that be nice?"

Olivia cheered up at that thought. It would be nice to know another girl in fifth grade. She pictured her and Hayley being the best of friends, eating lunch together, pushing each other on the swings and playing hopscotch at recess, and having sleepovers. Olivia smiled.

"That would be really cool, Grandma. Does she like Pioneer Girl dolls?"

"Well, I don't know, Honey. I've never met her but I am sure you two will have something in common. She can show you around."

When Grandma finished, Olivia had two perfectly formed French braids going down her back, tied with mismatched rubber bands at the ends. Olivia noticed the two different colors, but she didn't mind. The Olivia staring back at her in the mirror looked different from the same old Olivia who normally wore a single ponytail. Grandma was the best hairdresser in the world.

Olivia wondered if Hayley wore French braids.

Two

"My mission—to make God loved—will begin after my death. I will spend my heaven doing good on earth. I will send a shower of roses."
—St. Thérèse

It was the day before Olivia's dad would come to take Olivia back home on the airplane, and Grandma Rosemary's house was quiet. Olivia thought maybe Grandma was taking a nap, so she took one of her favorite books out onto the back porch and settled into one of the wicker chairs for a good read. It was warm and comfortable out on Grandma's sunny back porch. She was just starting a new chapter when Grandma came outside with a little pink box in her hand.

"What are you reading?"

"It's a book about some kids who lived during the Civil War," Olivia said.

"I don't mean to interrupt, but I have something special for you."

Olivia looked up with interest and put her book down on the side table.

When Grandma gave her the box, Olivia held it in her hands and looked down at it. It looked very old and the corners were not sharp but rubbed away. The pink color was faded and worn. On the lid was a drawing of a single rose.

Olivia opened the lid slowly. Nestled on a soft bed of tissue lay what looked like a bracelet.

"It's a pretty bracelet, Grandma," Olivia said as she held out her arm and tried it on her wrist.

"Oh no, Honey, it's not a bracelet," Grandma said as her soft, wrinkled fingers gently reached over and took it. "Why, it's a chaplet, Livvy."

Olivia tilted her head and studied it.

"What's a chaplet, Grandma?" Olivia had never seen one before.

"It's like a rosary, but smaller. You can use different chaplets to say different prayers. This one is for St. Thérèse, the Little Flower."

Olivia counted twenty-four pink beads, each in the shape of tiny roses. They were attached to a small gold medal with a picture of a pretty lady on it. "She looks just like the statue at church with the roses," Olivia noted. "Is that St. Thérèse too?"

"Yes. She is a very special friend to me and I think she could be a very special friend to you too, if you like."

Olivia went over to Grandma, who was sitting on the big wicker loveseat, and curled up next to her, putting her head on her lap. It felt cozy and safe, reminiscent of days when Olivia had done this all of the time, without reservation, when she was much younger. Today it just felt natural, even for an incoming fifth grader.

"Just like when you were little," Grandma said as she stroked Olivia's hair with her wrinkled hands.

"I wish I was little," Olivia murmured.

"That's exactly what St. Thérèse said over a hundred years ago. She said, 'I wish to be little.' She wanted to be a child in God's eyes because that is the way to get to Heaven."

Olivia turned her head to look at Grandma. "Tell me more about St. Thérèse, Grandma."

Grandma closed her eyes and a peaceful smile came over her face.

She began, "A long time ago in a village in France called Lisieux, a little girl lived with her father and her sisters. Her mother died when she was very young, but she managed to live a happy life. Thérèse was a very sweet, religious little girl who loved Jesus deeply. She used to pray to the Blessed Mother all of the time. She got very sick as a child and her family was worried and feared she would not get well, but a miracle happened and Thérèse was healed after she saw the Blessed Mother's statue smile down at her on her sickbed. She yearned for many years to become a Carmelite nun and finally got permission to enter the convent at a very young age—fifteen."

"While she was a nun living in the convent, she created her own special way of loving Jesus, and she called it her 'Little Way.'"

"What did she mean by that?" asked Olivia.

"Well," Grandma started, "Thérèse was a simple young woman, almost childlike. In fact, her formal name is St. Thérèse of the Child Jesus and the Holy Face. She believed that you can show your love for God by doing little things for Him with great love. It doesn't have to be a big, important thing like curing a disease or saving someone's life. Those are wonderful acts, too, but Thérèse teaches us that anyone can do something wonderful for God, no matter how little. Thérèse used to pray for a nun she lived with who was hard to get along with and wasn't very friendly to her. She also did her chores in the convent without complaining, even though sometimes she was tired and just didn't feel like it."

"Was Thérèse perfect?" Olivia wanted to know. She sure sounded perfect to her. And sometimes it's kind of hard to like people who are perfect.

"Oh no," laughed Grandma. "When she was a young girl, she was much like you are, and had worries and doubts about the future just like you and me. She didn't like school because the girls would tease her. Sometimes she'd nod off while praying! That used to embarrass her. She was quite precocious and stubborn. She used to have temper tantrums and hit her sister Céline. She always felt very remorseful after she did those things and would run to her parents and apologize profusely. But she was special because she prayed from her heart and showed God her love for others in the most simple ways. She wants us to follow those simple ways—her Little Way."

"What do you mean by 'simple ways'?" asked Olivia.

"Oh, like a smile for someone who is feeling sad, or doing something you don't want to do but know you should. Being nice to people who aren't nice to you, or not complaining about something like when you have a sore throat or have to make your bed, or do a chore when it's not your turn to do it, things like that. She taught us that doing those kinds of simple deeds are graceful things we do for our love of God.

"One time in the convent she got into trouble for breaking a vase. She didn't even do it, but she kept that fact to herself. She didn't argue about it, but instead got down on her knees and begged for forgiveness. She knew it would make God happy. She never complained about the food in the convent; she'd even eat the worst meals. The nuns would give her leftover fish heads and say, 'Give it to Thérèse, she won't complain.' She did these things because love is so important to her."

"Why do people call her 'The Little Flower'?"

"Oh, Thérèse just adored flowers. She even said that she wanted to be like a little flower at God's feet, so He could look down at her and be pleased by her littleness and the simple, good things that she did to make God happy. Olivia, do you know that Thérèse got very sick and died a young woman? And that she wrote her life story in a book when she was sick, even though she did not feel well enough to write? One of the things she wrote in that book was this:

> After my death, I will let fall a shower of roses. I will
> spend my heaven doing good upon earth. I will raise
> up a mighty host of little saints. My mission is to make
> God loved...

"She promised that she would spend all of her time in Heaven doing good things for people so they could come to love God as she does."

For a while, Grandma and Olivia were quiet as Olivia thought about all she had heard. She could hear the sounds of two squirrels chasing each other in the back yard and the wind blowing the leaves in the big maple tree. The sky was starting to get dark and there was dampness in the air.

"But why roses?" asked Olivia after a long time.

"Because in her room, when she was sick, she would spend a lot of time praying and looking out the window at a beautiful rosebush, her favorite flower."

Grandma went on to explain that right after Thérèse went to Heaven, roses started to appear to those who had prayed to her. Sometimes it wasn't even a real rose, but the strong, beautiful scent of one. And sometimes it was just a reassuring feeling that Thérèse had heard their prayers. Grandma explained that it is

God who ultimately answers our prayers, but saints can pray to God on our behalf.

"Many, many people pray to St. Thérèse and I am one of them. I hope you will be too, Livvy. She is such a good friend to me and wants to help you with everything. She wants you to ask her for help and to trust God that everything will be okay."

"I know what, Grandma! I am going to ask Thérèse for a rose for me. If I see a rose, I'll know that Thérèse will answer my prayer to like my new school."

Grandma hesitated. "Livvy, the thing is, when you ask Thérèse for help, she may send a rose right away, but then again, she might not. If she decides in her own good time that you receive one unexpectedly, that is just wonderful. But many times people don't receive a rose in the way that you think."

"What do you mean, Grandma?"

"Well, sometimes people pray to St. Thérèse and if they don't see a rose right away, then they get frustrated. They think she hasn't heard them and isn't helping them, and that is just not true at all. She's listening; she's always listening."

Olivia was confused. Her grandma chuckled gently.

"Let me tell you a story. When I was a young woman, I prayed to St. Thérèse to help me find a nice man to marry who believed in God. I prayed to her for nine days, which is called a *novena*. I asked her to ask God to help me find this man. Well, you can bet that I thought that on the tenth day, a handsome young man would walk right up to my door and propose to me! It took three years for Thérèse to answer my prayer. Three years!"

"Did you think she forgot about you or wasn't listening?"

"Well, I did at the time, I am sorry to say. But I kept thinking of Thérèse's Little Way, and so I tried to be patient. It was not easy. My close girlfriends were getting married and having families and I was feeling left behind and sad. Sometimes I was even jealous. But Thérèse's Little Way kept coming back to me. So I put a smile on my face even though I was sad inside. I helped my friends with their weddings and babysat their babies when they became mothers. I kept hoping that someday, some way, I'd receive a rose as a sign from Thérèse.

"But looking back I can say that it all happened the way it was supposed to. Your grandpa wasn't even living in the same state as me when I first asked Thérèse to help me. But I believe she made it possible for your grandpa to come to Michigan and finally meet me. It was all happening behind the scenes, but I just couldn't see it. Do you know what I mean, Honey?"

Olivia thought she did, but she still felt confused about praying for a rose. Gentle raindrops started to fall on the metal roof of the back porch, making a pinging sound.

"You just have to trust St. Thérèse. You can ask her for help but you have to wait until her timing is right. Only she—and God—know best when that time is. Many times a rose turns up when you least expect it."

"Did you get a rose, Grandma?"

Grandma smiled, and a little tear appeared to glisten in her eye.

"As a matter of fact, I did. I was working in a dress shop when a young woman I did not know named Rita came in to pick up a dress that had been altered. I had never seen the dress before because I had not been the one to work on it and it was all wrapped up in a white dress bag. It was very late and I was working alone. I was just about to close the store when she arrived. Rita opened her purse and saw that her wallet was empty. She was very upset that she could not pay for the dress and take it home because she needed to wear it that same evening to a party. So she begged me to keep the shop open while she ran back home to get some money. I was a little nervous to do that, since the owner of the store had told me that I must close up the shop promptly at six o'clock. I did not want to get into trouble with my boss, but I felt so sorry for Rita that I bent the rules for her.

"I waited and waited for Rita to show up. She took a long time. It started to get dark and I was getting a little nervous. While I waited, I was curious, so to pass the time, I opened up the dress bag to take a peek at the dress she had said she simply had to have that night. It was a white lace gown with tiny red rosebuds all over it. It was quite beautiful. Just as I was peeking into the bag, the door opened with a jingle and into the store walked a very nice-looking young man. It was her brother Frank who had come to pick up the dress for his sister…"

Olivia felt a shiver run up her spine. She knew it wasn't from the drop in temperature that the rainstorm had brought. It was definitely something more! "Grandpa?" yelled Olivia excitedly.

"That's right, Honey. It was your grandpa. We talked and talked for so long we forgot about the time. Eventually it became too dark for me to walk home safely by myself, so your grandpa, ever the gentleman, walked me to my house and the rest is history."

"And those rosebuds on the dress…those must have been sent by St. Thérèse!" cried Olivia.

"I believe with all of my heart that they were."

"Your poor Great-Aunt Rita," sighed Grandma. "By the time your grandpa got home with that dress, it was too late to wear it! Boy, was she hopping mad!"

Olivia giggled and hugged Grandma close. Then the two of them closed the windows on the back porch and headed inside.

Three

"You know well enough that Our Lord does not look so much at the greatness of our actions, nor even at their difficulty, but at the love with which we do them."
—St. Thérèse

The next day, Olivia's dad flew in from Houston. He stopped by the house her mom and dad had bought earlier in the summer to check on things. Dad had brought a few suitcases of clothing and some delicate things they didn't want the movers to take.

He stayed in Grandma's other spare bedroom and they ordered pizza from Vinnie's that night: mushrooms and pineapple, just the way Olivia liked it. Grandma had made a big salad and some lemonade and the three of them sat around Grandma's big kitchen table and talked about the upcoming move. The family had four weeks to pack the rest of their things and get ready. Grandma offered to clean the house a few days before they arrived. Olivia thought Grandma was the best housecleaner around. Whenever it was Olivia's turn to sweep the kitchen floor or dust tables, she'd do it quickly just to get it over with. But Grandma would always do a slow, thorough job when she cleaned.

One time that summer when Olivia was helping Grandma dust

the living room, she asked her why she took her time when if you hurried, you could finish that much faster.

"Oh Livvy, if something is worth doing, it's worth doing the right way," Grandma had said.

After everyone had cleaned up the kitchen from dinner and Dad and Grandma were sitting out on the back porch, Olivia went to her room to pack the last of her things. Into the suitcase went some books and coloring books. The rest of the things like her toothbrush and stuffed panda bear, Fuzzy, would have to go in at the last minute tomorrow before they left. She looked around the room to see if there was anything else left to put in the suitcase.

She didn't want to leave Grandma's house. She had had such a fun vacation and now it was at an end. And going back to Houston for the last time was sad, too. She thought of having to say goodbye to Claire and Emily. It would be horrible. She wondered if any of them would cry, or if they would try to laugh it off so nobody would be upset.

Olivia herself felt sad. Going back to Texas tomorrow meant one thing: facing the fact that they'd be leaving. Packing boxes. Cleaning out her room for the final time. She wondered what the house would look like on the day of the move. Probably all empty and lonely looking. Olivia sighed. Suddenly she herself felt very lonely.

She raised her hand to bite her fingernails, her worst habit, and stopped herself. If she kept that up, her fingernail would get all sore and bleed. It hurt a lot when she bit it too far down. She needed something else to do with her fingers. She looked around the room.

On the top of the dresser, Olivia spied the box Grandma had given her with the St. Thérèse chaplet inside. She opened it up and sat on the bed, holding it in her hands. She could hear the soft murmur of Grandma's and Dad's voices out on the back porch, Grandma chuckling at something Dad had said.

"St. Thérèse is your friend forever. You can talk to her anytime you want. She wants to help you."

Grandma's words entered Olivia's mind. She pursed her lips together and began,

St. Thérèse, you don't know me, but my name is Olivia Thomas. I'm ten years old and in a month I'll be leaving Texas to live here in Michigan. I'm a pretty good girl…well, most of the time. I help Mom with my baby sister Lucy. Sometimes I don't like to do what I'm told. I guess I have what is called a stubborn streak. And my temper…well, let's just say that I could use a little work in that area.

I get mostly good grades, except in handwriting, which is pretty sloppy according to my teachers in Texas. I just don't see the point in having perfect handwriting, I guess. Oh, and math. I'm pretty much a C student in math.

I don't want to move, St. Thérèse. Did you ever move? Oh, that's right; Grandma told me all about you and she said you moved to a place called

Lisieux after your mom died. You were only four when that happened. I am sorry your mom died, St. Thérèse. My gramps died two years ago. Do you ever see him in Heaven? Please tell him we miss him very much. I don't even eat tuna fish anymore because it makes me miss him more.

Daddy says we'll like it here, and that my new school is nice. Grandma has a new friend named Hayley for me to meet. Please make her nice. Please ask God to help me fit in there. Please, if you will, send me a rose to let me know everything will be okay.

And St. Thérèse? Thanks for being my new friend.

She fingered the pink chaplet and closed her eyes. What was it Grandma had said? Twenty-four rose beads to represent the twenty-four years of St. Thérèse's life. One *Our Father* on the medal. That was easy enough; she'd memorized that in kindergarten:

Our Father,
Who art in Heaven
Hallowed be Thy name.

Thy Kingdom come,
Thy will be done,
On Earth as it is in Heaven.

Give us this day our daily bread,
And forgive us our trespasses
As we forgive those who trespass against us
And lead us not into temptation
But deliver us from evil.
Amen.

Olivia fingered the medal with the image of St. Thérèse on it. It was bumpy and felt good when she rubbed it with her finger. Now—what did Grandma say was next? Oh yes, a *Glory Be*. Olivia closed her eyes again and tried to concentrate really hard. She was a little nervous. This was her first time doing this. She had prayed the rosary before, but that was in school with the entire class and her teacher leading, not alone.

Glory Be to the Father, and to the Son, and to the Holy Spirit.

As it was in the beginning, is now and ever shall be,

World without end.

Amen.

This was to be followed by "St. Thérèse of the Child Jesus, pray for us."

Olivia took a deep breath.

St. Thérèse of the Child Jesus,

Pray for us.

Olivia's fingers traveled to the next bead. She repeated what she had said on the first bead. Easy. She went on to the next one. And the next one. She got sidetracked a couple of times. Her mind wandered to something else she wanted to add to her suitcase, or the fact that she was getting thirsty. She tried to shake off those thoughts and got back on track. Soon she had said the two prayers on each of the twenty-four beads. Her fingers met the medal again and she knew she had finished.

Olivia's eyes flew open. She did it! She prayed St. Thérèse's chaplet for the very first time. She felt an unexplainable feeling of peace come over her.

With a smile on her face, she went to the bathroom to brush her teeth and put on her pajamas before bed.

Four

*"To Call God my Father and to Know myself His Child,
that is Heaven to me...."*
—*St. Thérèse*

Olivia stirred her sticky oatmeal around in circles with her spoon. She wasn't hungry this morning. Her stomach was in knots, and she felt what must be butterflies fluttering inside. *I wonder whoever came up with that saying,* she thought. *Butterflies in your stomach. It means you're nervous. But butterflies are so beautiful. How could they be compared to the uncomfortable feeling of being anxious?*

She hated feeling nervous, but she couldn't help it. Today was the first day of fifth grade at her new school. Two big things in one day. She thought of all of the other kids at St. Michael's School who were probably eating their breakfasts at the same time as she. They were lucky. They would be able to see all of their old friends. They would know their way around the hallways, know where to go for lunch, be able to find the bathrooms and drinking fountains. She'd be lost in a sea of new faces and new rules.

Even the uniforms were different. She looked down sadly at her white and blue plaid skirt. In fourth grade at her old school in Texas, it was so warm that they got to wear navy blue walking shorts and tennis shoes. But as Olivia swung her legs with her new brown shoes, she felt a little better. She loved these new shoes and had had such fun picking them out with her mom and her baby sister Lucy last week at the mall. Afterward her mom had treated her to a strawberry milkshake at the ice cream shop in town.

"Olivia? Aren't you hungry, Honey?" her mom asked as she put Lucy in the high chair and opened a jar of baby pears. Lucy banged her pudgy hands on her tray in anticipation.

Mrs. Thomas looked worried as she snapped on Lucy's bib.

"It's the first day of school and you need to have some food in your tummy," she said.

"I know, Mama," moaned Olivia. "But I'm just not hungry." She held her stomach and made a face. "The butterflies are in there flying around and there's no room for oatmeal."

Mrs. Thomas giggled. "I know. I remember how it was on the first day of school."

Just then Mr. Thomas came into the kitchen.

"Well, well, look at my little Olivia in her new uniform. Big day, huh?" He poured coffee into his travel mug and took a sip.

"Yeah, I guess," said Olivia slowly.

"You guess?" her dad asked. He went over to Olivia's chair and kissed the top of her head. "We just moved in a week ago. I know it's a lot all at once. Give it some time."

"She's a little nervous, that's all," said her mom as she wiped a sticky mess of oatmeal and pears off of Lucy's chin with the edge of her bib.

Lucy sure is a messy eater, Olivia thought. She guessed all babies were that way.

"You'll be fine, Livvy. I know you'll like your new school a lot. Lots of friendly kids and teachers." He looked at her sad face. "Cheer up. Grandma knows of a nice girl named Hayley you can meet. We'll bake some muffins or something tonight after dinner, okay? There's a new recipe I've been wanting to try with you." Mr.

Thomas was an excellent cook and had passed the love of cooking on to Olivia, who had become quite a good cook in her ten years. Her favorite thing to do with her dad was to spend time with him in the kitchen, experimenting with different bread recipes, learning how to separate an egg, and kneading homemade pizza dough. Her mom liked to joke that she had two professional chefs in the house.

"But try to eat a couple more spoonfuls so we can go, though. We don't want you to be late on your first day!"

Olivia put a spoonful of lukewarm oatmeal into her mouth and forced her teeth to chew.

Before she knew it she was out the door with her brand new pink backpack and lunchbox. "Have a great day, Sugar!" her mom yelled as she left through the back door.

I'll try, she thought. She looked at Lucy, all happy and sticky from pears and milk. Lucky Lucy. She could stay home all day with Mom. *She* didn't have to go to a new school and meet new people and learn new stuff. Babies were lucky. Olivia would have given anything to shrink back down to being a baby again. Ah, to be little! She didn't know how good she had it then!

They walked to the garage. As Olivia started to buckle her seat belt, she stopped and gasped. How could she have forgotten?

"Wait!" she cried to her dad, who was just getting into the front seat. "I need to go back and get something!"

Her dad sighed. "Okay, but try to hurry, Pumpkin. You don't want to miss the first bell."

"Sorry, Daddy!"

Olivia ran inside past her startled mother at the kitchen table. Her feet pounded the stairs as she burst into her room. She stood in the middle of the room and looked around in a panic. There were moving boxes everywhere.

Olivia tripped over a box of half-clothed Pioneer Girl dolls.

Where was it? If she didn't find it, there was no way she could face going to school. The butterflies would never go away.

Was it in her nightstand?

The drawer was empty.

Her desk drawers?

Nope. Filled with pencil shavings, stickers, crayons, and old coloring books. Breathlessly, she threw open her closet doors and began tossing out shoes and clothes.

"Olivia?" Her mom called from the bottom of the stairs. "Your father's waiting. Hurry *up!*"

Olivia bit her forefinger, her worst bad habit, and peeled off the nail. She had promised herself and God she would stop this habit, but she was desperate and needed to think. Where was it in all of this mess? WHERE?

"Livvy!" Her mom's tone was sharp now.

Frustrated, Olivia turned and left her messy room and bounded down the stairs.

"You're going to be late! Did you find what you were looking for?"

"NO!" Olivia shouted too harshly, as she ran into the garage where her dad was waiting. She instantly felt bad for being rude to her mom. There was that temper of hers flaring up again.

Sigh. *I'll have to make up for that later*, she thought as she buckled her seat belt and the car backed down the driveway.

She leaned her head against the car window and closed her eyes. "St. Thérèse," she prayed silently, "I sure wish I had your chaplet. Please help me have a good day at this new school."

Her finger traveled up into her mouth and she bit a nail down to the quick, thinking of her precious item. There was absolutely no way she could start fifth grade and St. Michael's without it.

Five

*"Offer God the sacrifice of never gathering
any fruit off your tree."*
—St. Thérèse

"Chad O' Toole?"

"Here!" A short, redheaded boy named Chad yelled a little too loudly, making Olivia jump in her seat. He turned and grinned back at Olivia, who was seated in back of him in the third row. He studied Olivia for a second and then reached up with his fingers and pulled up his eyelids.

Olivia scowled. Boys could be so gross!

"A lower octave will do, Chad, and turn around and face the front please," said Mrs. Wells as she peered at him over her reading glasses. Mrs. Wells was a young woman with strawberry blonde hair. *Too young for reading glasses*, thought Olivia as she studied her new teacher. Her long hair was swept off her shoulders and done up in a tortoise-shell clip.

To Olivia, she was absolutely the most beautiful teacher she had ever seen. She thought back to last year's teacher at her old school: Mrs. Bardsley. Old Mrs. Bardsley, with the salt-and-pepper hair in a bob, who shuffled rather than walked, and always wore the same color every day: black. Black skirts, black sweaters, black slacks. Maybe a colored blouse thrown in for good measure, but always with black. Mrs. Bardsley was a sweet lady, though. She always had time for a hug and treated everyone fairly. Everyone loved her, but she wasn't what you would call glamorous.

Not like Mrs. Wells. Olivia wondered if she had ever been Miss America. But that seemed like a silly question. How could that be, when Mrs. Wells was a *teacher*?

On her left ring finger, a white gold diamond ring sparkled brightly. Mrs. Wells wore makeup: bright pink lipstick and softly shaded eyes. Her dangly topaz bracelet matched the rest of her outfit.

"Sabrina Pearson?"

"Here!" piped up a perky voice from the front seat in row four.

"Zachary Seever?"

"Mrs. Wells? He's sick with a bad cold," offered Chad in a lower voice this time.

In the back of the room, Olivia heard a low snicker. She wondered why someone would laugh that this boy Zachary was sick today.

"On the first day of school? What a shame," said Mrs. Wells as she wrote something on the attendance sheet with her red pen.

Olivia looked around the classroom as Mrs. Wells did the roll call. It was a very old building, unlike her old school in Texas that had just been recently built.

St. Michael's was made of cinderblocks and older windows, although Dad told her that the school had just made improvements and modernized the library and other parts of the building.

In the corner of the room, on a little pedestal, stood a statue of Mary, her arms open wide in her blue mantle, as if she were giving Olivia a hug.

"Don't worry, Olivia," Mary seemed to reassure Olivia from her shelf. "You'll be just fine."

The rest of the room was all dressed up for the first day of school. There were nametags on each of the desks, written in the perfect cursive handwriting only an elementary school teacher could have. A giant calendar for the month of September was on the wall, with an apple cutout for each day. A huge banner decorated with all kinds of cartoon shoes hung above the whiteboard, proclaiming, "I will walk with Jesus!" Centered at the top of the wall above the whiteboard was a large crucifix.

Olivia decided it was a comforting, happy classroom. Lots of things to look at if you got bored or wanted to daydream, which happened quite frequently to Olivia in school, unfortunately.

"Hayley Stewart?"

Olivia's head jerked away from the Blessed Mother statue. Hayley. Wasn't that the name of the girl Grandma had told her about? The one who was supposed to be her new friend?

"Here, Mrs. Wells," offered a high-pitched girl's voice from the back of the room in back of Sabrina's seat.

Hayley took the rubber band out of her long blonde hair, shook it out, and redid her ponytail. She leaned in to Sabrina. The two whispered something and started to giggle.

"Olivia Thomas?"

Olivia raised her hand shyly. So shyly, in fact, that her teacher could not see her do it.

"Olivia?"

Olivia raised her hand a little higher this time.

"Oh, my. I didn't even see you! Olivia, please come up to the front of the room so I can introduce you properly," Mrs. Wells said, her teeth all showing in a hearty smile.

Olivia got out of her seat and walked up the long, straight aisle to the front of the room to stand next to Mrs. Wells. She turned to face twenty-five faces who curiously studied the new student.

Mrs. Wells put a protective arm around Olivia's shoulders. She smelled like coconut skin lotion.

"Class, I'd like you to meet our new student, Olivia Thomas. She comes to us from Houston, Texas. Right over here," she motioned to the large wall map of the United States behind her desk. With a perfectly painted pink fingernail, she pointed to the state of Texas and slid her finger down until she reached the bold letters **HOUSTON**.

"Olivia was born and raised in Texas but just moved here to Michigan this summer. Welcome to St. Michael's, Olivia. Class, what do you say to welcome our new student to Room 20?"

"Wel-come O-liv-ia," the class chanted slowly.

Mrs. Wells, obviously pleased, patted Olivia on the back. She looked at Olivia in expectation.

"Um, thanks ma'am," she said and then turned to face the class.

"And thanks, y'all."

In the back of row one, a low chorus of giggles ensued again.

Olivia cleared her throat. Time to get back to her desk. She hurried to her seat and sat down, red-faced. Who giggled? She looked around the room to see if she could figure it out, but deep down she knew. It had come from the direction of Hayley and Sabrina, she was sure of it. She felt a lump in her throat and wished for her St. Thérèse chaplet, wherever it was.

In front of her, Chad turned around and gave her a huge grin. "You talk kinda funny," he whispered.

Olivia looked at him and made a face.

"Well, you look funny," she answered, and instantly felt guilty. But she didn't like this new boy Chad. She guessed he was a troublemaker. There was one in every class. At her old school it was Travis Butler, the popular class clown. He had gotten into trouble for pulling the fire alarm and had to stay home from school for a whole week. Olivia had been forced to sit by him for the entire school year.

Chad just continued his silly grin and turned around to face the front.

Olivia hoped Mrs. Wells would make up a new seating chart. She didn't want anything to do with Chad. One school year with a kid like Travis was enough.

Mrs. Wells went through the rest of roll call and then the class stood up to say the Pledge of Allegiance. After that, everyone made the sign of the cross and said the morning prayer that Mrs. Wells had written on the whiteboard.

Our dear God,

Please bless us on this first day of fifth grade. Please help us to learn a lot this year, make new friends, and enjoy our holy school. Thank you for St. Michael's School, our principal Sister Anne Marie, and all of the students and teachers. We pray this in our Lord Jesus' name.

Amen.

Olivia felt something land on her shoe and looked down at her feet under her desk. It was a little piece of paper. She looked up at Mrs. Wells, who was busy at the whiteboard with her back turned, writing down the classroom rules for the year.

Slowly she opened the folded paper.

Hi. Want to eat lunch with us???

Olivia folded the note back and hid it under her new pencil box. She looked around the room. Who wrote the note?

Then she saw Hayley and Sabrina to her left with grins on their faces. Sabrina did a little wave. Olivia waved back. How great! Friends already and she'd only been at her new school for twenty minutes.

Six

"Nothing is done well when it is done out of self-interest."
—St. Thérèse

The rest of the morning went by in a blur: reviewing times tables in math, practicing cursive, and learning new spelling words. Olivia was exhausted by the time lunch rolled around at 12:30. Mrs. Wells dismissed the class to their coat hooks to get their lunchboxes and head down to the cafeteria. Olivia reached into her backpack and pulled out her new Pioneer Girl lunchbox.

"Hi there," said a voice behind her. Startled, Olivia turned around and was face to face with Hayley. "I'm Hayley. My grandma told me about you."

"Hi," said Olivia. She smiled shyly.

"Want to eat lunch with me and Sabrina?"

"Um, sure. But I don't know where the cafeteria is."

"Oh, we'll show you. Come on, Sabrina," she cried carelessly to Sabrina, who was exiting the classroom. "You're taking too long and I'm starving!"

"Hi...Olivia, is it? Is that a Pioneer Girl lunchbox you have?" asked Sabrina with a wry smile as she joined the two. She nudged Hayley.

"It's cute," said Hayley. "I had one of those in third grade. But it's a little babyish," she said as she held up her plain red lunchbox. Sabrina tapped her lunchbox with her finger. "See? No design, or just a simple one. You're in fifth grade now. Come on, let's go."

Olivia suddenly felt very embarrassed by her Pioneer Girl lunchbox. It was a present from Grandma and she had loved it when they had seen it at the store. It was more expensive than some of the other lunchboxes. Grandma had bought it for her on the spot.

"You don't have to use your allowance," Grandma had said as she saw the look of longing on Olivia's face. "Let me buy it for you."

"No, Grandma, that's okay." Grandma was on a fixed income and didn't have lot of extra money to buy expensive things, Olivia knew.

"A new lunchbox for a new school," Grandma had insisted, and took the lunchbox from Olivia's hands.

Suddenly it looked very out of place here.

At lunch, the children sat down at long tables and said grace, led by Sister Anne Marie, a petite lady of about sixty with glasses on a string.

Olivia sat directly across from the two girls. At this point Hayley decided it was time she told Olivia a little bit about herself.

"I've been going to St. Michael's since kindergarten," she said proudly. "So I know everything about this school. I have one older brother named Ryan who goes to high school at St. Luke's. He used to terrorize me but my mom finally put a stop to it and grounded him. He babysits me after school when my mom's at work, and we watch PG-13 movies," she bragged.

Wow. Olivia was only allowed to watch G movies, and once in a while a PG movie if her parents thought it was okay. She decided it would be in her best interest to keep that little fact to herself. She wondered why Hayley hadn't mentioned her dad.

Next it was Sabrina's turn. "I have an older sister in eighth grade," said Sabrina. "She's a pain, so I go through her stuff when she's not home. She keeps a diary and she's always writing about this boy named Kyle who she has a crush on!"

Sabrina and Hayley laughed hard at this.

"*If only Kyle would talk to me! He's so cute in his football uniform!*" Sabrina mocked.

The two girls exploded in a chorus of giggles. This time, Olivia joined in, just to fit in. After all, it felt weird to be the only one not laughing.

Olivia didn't think it was very nice of Sabrina to be reading her sister's private thoughts, but she said nothing. She so wanted to make new friends, and these girls were nice enough to include her. She didn't want to rock the boat. And she really wanted to fit in.

"What bad luck that you have to sit behind Chad," Hayley said with a roll of her eyes. "He's such a geek."

"Oh, I know!" exclaimed Sabrina. "He's going to torment you until December, when Mrs. Wells lets us change seats. With his weird faces and jokes. He thinks he's so funny."

"Does he get in trouble a lot?" Olivia wanted to know.

"Not really. The teachers like him. I think they feel sorry for him," Sabrina said. "I can see why—he hardly has any friends!"

"What about that metal-mouth Jenna?" Hayley corrected Sabrina.

"Oh yeah, her. Whatever," Sabrina dismissed her name with a wave of her hand as she stabbed a straw into her milk carton.

Olivia suddenly felt sorry for this boy who she had originally thought was a carbon copy of Travis.

"Why doesn't he have any friends?"

Hayley jumped in. "Like I said, he's a geek. Can't you tell? He's just...weird. His uniform pants are always worn out and faded. They're always too short, even in September. He's got that crazy red hair. And I heard he lives in some ancient house that's about ready to fall down!"

"He has the dumbest science fair projects," Sabrina put in. "What was the one he did last year?" Sabrina turned to Hayley.

Hayley practically jumped out of her seat. "Oh! It had to do with his pet tree frog Jumper! He demonstrated how he feeds it tiny crickets every morning. And he imitated how it croaks at night, like this!" and she let out a loud, deep-throated frog noise.

Sabrina laughed hard and slapped her hand on the lunch table. "Oh yeah! And he was so serious about it!"

The two girls exploded into laughter. Olivia felt uncomfortable. She'd had enough of them making fun of Chad, even if he did make gross faces at her in class.

She scanned the cafeteria, looking to see if it was really true, if Chad really didn't have any friends. Then she saw it: Chad sitting alone by himself at the end of a big table, eating a sandwich off of a paper plate. He looked sad and alone.

Olivia looked away, unable to watch. It made her uncomfortable.

"Tell us about you," urged Sabrina as she popped a few grapes in her mouth.

Olivia was glad they changed the subject. She unwrapped her sandwich and looked up, a thoughtful look on her face.

"Well, there's really not much to say," she said apologetically. "I'm kind of boring, actually. I have a baby sister Lucy who is really cute and talks a lot. We used to have a cat named Tweezer but then I found out that I was allergic, so we gave him to my cousin. We moved from Texas, which you know, and now," she shrugged, "here I am."

"What's it like in Texas?" asked Hayley between mouthfuls of strawberry yogurt.

"It's warm," said Olivia cautiously, not sure what Hayley wanted to hear.

"Do *y'all* have, like, cowboys riding around on horses on the street?" Sabrina asked and then laughed at her clever remark. When she laughed she let out a huge snort.

"Don't snort, Sabrina, it's really gross!" laughed Hayley.

It occurred to Olivia that Sabrina and Hayley laughed a lot. Maybe too much.

"Sure!" said Olivia, trying to sound like she wasn't hurt by Sabrina's remark.

"No way."

"Well," said Olivia, trying to backtrack. "I mean, at rodeos and at the stock show."

"What's a stock show?"

Olivia took a bite of her cheese sandwich and suddenly felt very tired. She really didn't feel like explaining what a stock show was. The girls would just laugh for the millionth time.

"It's a yearly event with lots of animals, contests, and barbecued food. But the main event is that the farmers bring their stock animals to show them off. It's a lot of fun." She tried to sound convincing. How to explain to a bunch of northern girls what a stock show was?

"Animals? If we had one here, Chad could bring his pet tree frog!" Sabrina cried, pleased at her own joke. Hayley nudged Sabrina in the side as she laughed. "Good one!"

The girls looked at Olivia as they laughed, and, out of nowhere, Olivia felt the urge to laugh with them. She knew making fun of Chad was wrong, but suddenly she felt exhausted trying to fit in at this new school. She needed friends in fifth grade, and Hayley and Sabrina were nice enough to let them sit with her and be their friend.

And maybe Chad *was* weird. Wasn't he? She thought back

to the way he stuck out his eyeballs. If Chad wanted to make friends, why would he do that to someone?

She glanced over at Chad again, who was standing up to return his tray and talking to a ponytailed girl she recognized from class. She didn't want to be like him, eating all alone and having people make fun of her.

Olivia turned to the girls and laughed loudly at Sabrina's joke. "Yeah, he could! Maybe he'd try to feed it barbecued crickets!"

Hayley looked approvingly at Olivia while Sabrina smiled. She had obviously said the right thing.

The cheese sandwich Olivia had eaten started to sit in her stomach like a rock. She felt a little sick.

Olivia noticed Hayley staring openly at her ears. Instinctively, she put her hand up to one of her earlobes.

"What?"

"Your ears aren't pierced," she said matter-of-factly. "I can tell."

Sabrina, too, took interest.

"I can't," replied Olivia, embarrassed.

"Oh, you can get them pierced," she assured her as if that solved the problem. "You just can't wear earrings to school. Sister Anne Marie's rules."

"No, I mean my parents won't let me. Not 'til I'm older."

"Why in the world not?" Hayley wanted to know. "*Everyone's* got pierced ears."

"I dunno," replied Olivia, growing more and more uncomfortable with this conversation. For crying out loud, no one had ever given her a hard time about it back home. Claire and Emily weren't even interested in pierced ears yet. When Lauren McKinley had gotten her ears pierced, they'd all shuddered at the thought of a sharp poke in the earlobes, especially when one of Lauren's earlobes had gotten infected and all scary looking.

The bell rang then, signaling that it was time to clean up and go back to class. The girls sipped the last of their milk and threw away their half-finished sandwiches.

"You don't still play with Pioneer Girls, do you?" Hayley wanted to know as they walked toward the cafeteria doors.

Olivia thought about how she, Emily, and Claire would spend hours in Claire's bedroom, making up far-fetched stories with their Pioneer Girl dolls. Just last month they'd made a house out of one of Olivia's spare moving boxes and had decorated it with leftover wallpaper and Claire's Pioneer Girl furniture. She hated leaving it behind with Claire.

"No," Olivia lied. "I've had this old thing for a long time. I really need to get a new one."

And with that Olivia tossed the empty lunchbox into a giant trash bin and walked with Sabrina and Hayley back to Room 20.

Seven

*"Without love, deeds, even the most brilliant,
count as nothing."*
—*St. Thérèse*

The playground at St. Michael's was small but had a large blue playscape that the children flocked to each day after lunch, buzzing around it like bees as they ran and climbed and chased each other on the wood chips, burning off energy they had bottled up all morning long. Olivia eyed the large bank of swings.

"Let's go swing!" she called to Hayley and Sabrina as she ran ahead to secure a swing for herself. They were going fast as hordes of girls headed in the same direction. Olivia wanted to be sure to get one.

Out of breath, she collapsed onto a black rubber swing and looked around as she started to swing and climb high, back and forth.

She looked for Hayley and Sabrina and noticed that they had decided to remain on the playscape. Olivia shrugged her shoulders and continued to swing higher, enjoying the sunshine, the warm September breeze, and the feeling of soaring like a bird into the sky.

"Hi," said the blonde girl in a ponytail on the swing next to her. "You're on my party line."

"Hmm?" asked Olivia, confused.

The girl laughed, showing a mouth full of metal and various orthodontia that Olivia was glad she didn't need yet. "That means we're swinging in synch," she explained. "Haven't you heard that one before?"

Olivia turned red. There was a lot she didn't seem to know: babyish lunchboxes, strange terms.

"Guess not," she said and smiled faintly.

"I'm Jenna," said the girl with the ponytail. "I'm in your class. I sit right by Mrs. Wells' desk."

Olivia took a closer look and remembered her talking to Chad at lunch. "I'm Olivia."

"I know," she said and laughed. "Mrs. Wells introduced you this morning, remember?" Olivia blushed again. Noticing, Jenna said, "That's okay. I was new here once too. Last year."

"Oh, really?"

"Yeah, I moved here from Massachusetts. They made fun of my accent, too." Jenna took one hand off of the chain and pointed in the direction of the playscape.

"Who did?"

"Lots of people," she said simply. "But only for a couple of months. Nobody notices anymore. Well, mostly nobody."

Olivia was silent. She guessed that meant Hayley and Sabrina, but she didn't want to ask. She didn't really want to know.

"Do you like St. Michael's?" Jenna wanted to know.

Olivia thought for a moment. "I do. I like Mrs. Wells and Sister Anne Marie. They're nice."

Jenna agreed. "We're lucky to have Mrs. Wells. She's the nicest teacher in the whole school. But they're all pretty nice here," she said. "Wait 'til you see the library. It was remodeled over the summer and we got a bunch of new books!"

"Really?" Olivia noted with interest as she swung higher into the sunshine. She loved to read. "Any cookbooks for kids?" She knew it was a long shot, but she had to ask.

"Yeah! In fact—"

From across the playground, Sabrina waved wildly to Olivia as she swung.

"Come over here!" she yelled from far away.

Olivia didn't want to. She was having a good time swinging and getting to know Jenna.

"Come ON, Olivia! We're playing a game!" joined in Hayley.

Olivia stopped pumping and started to slow her swing down.

"Are you always going to do what they say?" asked Jenna suddenly.

"No," said Olivia, slightly annoyed. "But they're my new friends." She felt defensive.

"Just be careful," said Jenna as she continued to swing back and forth. "Those two are trouble."

The swing slowed down enough for Olivia to jump off. When she landed on her two feet, she looked back at Jenna.

"Um…See ya," she called over her shoulder and ran off to join Hayley and Sabrina.

"Who were you talking to? I couldn't see," Hayley asked as soon as Olivia reached them.

"Jenna from class."

Hayley frowned. "Don't bother with her. She's weird," she said.

Sabrina nodded in agreement. "She's friends with Chad and some of the other nerds."

"She seemed nice," Olivia said.

"She's okay," Hayley said and then added, "but she's got the strangest hobbies. Like, one time for show-and-tell last year she brought in some weird red rubber baking dish that was all bendy. Remember, Sabrina?"

Sabrina's eyes got all wide. "Oh yeah! We were all like, 'What IS that?' Turned out it was something called—"

"Silicone?" piped up Olivia excitedly.

"Yeah," Sabrina said, surprised. "How did you know?"

"My dad and I use those. They're for baking. They're nonstick and really easy to clean."

Sabrina and Hayley stood still, and the three were quiet among the loud shouting of the children running around the playground.

Olivia looked down and awkwardly kicked a few wood chips with the toe of her shoe. "I like to cook," she said finally.

"Oh," said Hayley.

"Oh," echoed Sabrina.

Olivia's feelings were immediately hurt and once again she felt her temper starting to set in. Sabrina always sounded like a parrot to Hayley's comments. There was absolutely nothing wrong with having cooking as a hobby. After all, it was better than what these two girls had for a hobby: making fun of people and laughing at their own private jokes. She looked at Hayley and Sabrina and studied their smirky expressions. She felt a sudden urge to smack them both. She managed to suppress it. Certainly the Little Flower would have overcome the temptation, especially when she was in the fifth grade. Wouldn't she have?

"But I only cook once in a while," Olivia said hurriedly, eager to cover up what she had just said. Apparently it wasn't "cool" to Hayley and Sabrina. "You know, like around Christmas and stuff."

"Sure. Maybe you can make us something sometime," Hayley said vaguely.

"Um, yeah," Sabrina put in awkwardly.

Eager to change the subject, Olivia looked around for a distraction, and found one.

"Hey, what's Chad doing?"

Chad was sitting under a tree by himself. He seemed very engrossed in the book he was reading.

"I bet it's some boring, nerdy encyclopedia of disgusting bugs," Olivia said, trying to take the attention off herself.

She instantly felt horrible.

"Come on! Let's go see!" Hayley smiled wickedly.

The three girls ran across to where Chad was sitting. Hayley turned around and put her finger to her lips. "Shhh." She tiptoed behind Chad, grabbed the book out of his hands, and held it up for everyone to see.

"Hey!" yelled Chad angrily.

"*The Life of the American Tree Frog*!" Hayley read the title of the book with obvious glee. "Olivia, you were right!"

Hayley tossed the book to Sabrina, who held it high above her head.

"Give me back my book, Sabrina!" yelled Chad.

"Ha ha!" Sabrina held the book out of Chad's reach. She raced away from Chad, still holding his book high. Chad got up from the ground and started to chase her, but he was no match for Sabrina, who had long legs and ran swiftly.

"Come on, guys," Olivia said, rather lamely. She knew she

should be more persistent in telling them to stop. What was holding her back?

Hayley looked around cautiously to see where the recess moms were. Satisfied that they were way out of earshot, she laughed loudly. "Pass it to me, Sabrina!"

Sabrina threw the book into the air and Hayley caught it with outstretched hands. The three ran in circles, the girls trying to outrun Chad. Then Sabrina tossed it to Olivia, who had been standing by the tree, watching in shock.

Olivia stood still while she held Chad's book, unsure what to do with it. She felt the familiar butterflies come back to settle in her stomach. Her heart told her to give it back to Chad and apologize on behalf of Sabrina and Hayley. They'd embarrassed Chad enough. They should stop this.

Olivia, you know this is wrong. You're being cruel to Chad.

But St. Thérèse's words went unheard. The desire to please her new friends seemed to overtake her knowledge of right and wrong. One look at Hayley and Sabrina's wild eyes and expectant grins, and Olivia felt the uncontrollable urge to please them, to continue the cat-and-mouse game. For the life of her, she could not figure out why their acceptance was so important to her. It puzzled her greatly.

Chad stopped running, panting and out of breath. Sabrina and Hayley stopped, too, in anticipation of Olivia's next move.

Did she want to end up like Jenna, the new kid with the funny accent who was teased? A girl who swung alone at recess?

Or Chad, a boy who read by himself, ate lunch with Jenna or alone most days, and was the object of Hayley and Sabrina's lunchtime conversations?

She knew her answer. She didn't like it, but at that moment

she could not ignore the expectant faces of Hayley and Sabrina.

With a small grin, she held *The Life of the American Tree Frog* up and flung it Frisbee-style in the direction of the street. It soared over the grass and landed with a thud-like skid onto the road. The book lay on the pavement for a moment until a silver minivan came rumbling by and flattened it, fluttering the pages into the sky until they fell back down like a snow shower of colored paper, littering the street.

Olivia stood and stared unbelievingly at what she had just done.

"Olivia, what an arm!" yelled Hayley as she ran up to join her. Admiration was written all over Hayley's jubilant face. "Awesome throw!"

Speechless, Olivia turned around and felt hot with shame as she noticed Chad's face, wet from tears.

Eight

"When we accept our disappointment at our failures, God
immediately returns to us."
—St. Thérèse

That night, as Olivia lay in bed, she thought about Hayley
and Sabrina and Mrs. Wells. She thought about Chad and his tree
frog book and Jenna and the lunchbox she had thrown away—her
brand-new lunchbox that Grandma had bought her as a treat.

What a day. So many things had happened, most of them terrible things.

What would Mom and Dad say? she thought. *And what would
Grandma say about the lunchbox?* The thought of Grandma
knowing that hurt her most. She tried to shake the thought from
her mind. She simply could not tell her parents. They already
knew she had lost her St. Thérèse chaplet, and Mom wasn't too
thrilled when she heard the news.

"I hope you find it, Livvy. That was a very special gift from
Grandma. Her mother—your great grandmother—gave it to her."

"I know, Mom. I feel horrible."

Mom tucked the covers all around her and planted a kiss on
her forehead.

"I know you do. Time for prayers."

Every night since she could remember, Olivia said her prayers with her mom or dad at her bedside. But this night, for the very first time, she wanted to say them privately.

"Mom? Is it okay if I don't say them out loud tonight? I have some things I want to talk to God about that are private."

Her mother looked surprised and didn't say anything for a quick moment as she sat on the edge of Olivia's bed.

"Of course, Sugar. I understand." She smoothed the top of Olivia's head. "I guess you're getting older now." She gave her a quick kiss. "I've always enjoyed listening to you say your prayers, but I know that some things are private between you and God. Don't forget that you can always talk to Mama and Daddy too about anything. I'll leave you to your prayers."

"Thanks, Mama."

"I love you. Nighty night," she said as she turned on Olivia's nightlight and turned off her bedside lamp. "I'm glad you like your new school," she said from the doorway.

"Me too, Mama," said Olivia in the darkness.

"Don't worry about the chaplet. I'll look for it tonight, okay? It has to be around the house somewhere in all of this stuff."

"Okay, Mom."

She hugged Fuzzy tightly to her chest as she thought about what she wanted to say. First she talked to Jesus and told him everything. Then she called on St. Thérèse.

Hi St. Thérèse,

Well, I'm sure you saw what happened today. I threw away the lunchbox Grandma got me. I feel terrible about it. I really, really wish I hadn't done that. I was just trying to make Hayley and Sabrina like me. I am sure they are nice girls once you get to know them. But Hayley can be kind of mean sometimes. And of course you know what happened with Chad and his book.

Oh St. Thérèse, why did I do that? I've never done anything as bad as that in my whole life. I made fun of him, too. I did so many bad things in one day. All on my first day of school. Please ask God to help me be a good girl, St. Thérèse. And please help me find your chaplet. It's missing. I know I don't need it to pray to you, but Grandma gave it to me and it's very special.

Amen.

Olivia rolled over in bed and faced her darkened window. She heard a car pass by outside in the front of the house. She was still getting used to all of the strange noises in the new house; different creaks the house made. The sound of her parents on the steps, or Lucy's muffled cry from her bedroom. Everything was so new and different here. She supposed it would just take time, like her mom and dad had said.

She rolled over again, trying to get comfortable. She knew with all her heart that she had let St. Thérèse down, and more importantly, had let God down. She knew that would make St. Thérèse sad. It was just so hard to be good all of the time, to do the right thing. Like with Hayley and Sabrina. On one hand, making new friends was a good thing, an honorable thing. But if it was at the cost of hurting someone else and being mean, suddenly it wasn't so good anymore. God would never want her to make new friends at the expense of someone else's feelings. And deep down, she knew that He would not want her to hang around girls who treated others poorly.

> St. Thérèse, it's me again. I want to make you happy. I want to make God happy. Your Little Way made God happy. Maybe it can work for me, too. Please help me follow your Little Way each day. Starting first thing tomorrow, that is what I am going to do. Please guide me so I do little things with great love.
>
> Amen.

It was then that her bare foot brushed against something under the covers at the foot of her bed. Olivia threw the covers off and reached for it. It was dark, so it was hard to tell what it was, but as soon as her fingers touched the object, she knew. It was her chaplet!

Could this be St. Thérèse's way of telling Olivia things were going to be okay? It had to be. She just knew it. St. Thérèse was telling her she could start fresh tomorrow. Tomorrow was a new day to please God, a new day to love.

Olivia smiled wide and held it up in the darkness.

"I found it, Mama! I found it!"

Nine

"Often just a word or friendly smile are enough..."
—St. Thérèse

Finding the St. Thérèse chaplet lifted a heavy burden off of Olivia's mind. She knew that St. Thérèse would hear her prayers even if she didn't have such a thing, of course, but it made her feel closer to her somehow. She liked to hold it in her hands when she talked to her, feel the bumpy rose beads and look at her picture on the medallion. Ever since Grandma had given her the chaplet a few weeks ago, she had used it to help her think of things to say to St. Thérèse. Besides, it helped her to practice the Our Father and the Glory Be by doing them in repetition.

The sound of rain on the roof woke Olivia up before her mom did. She lay in bed listening to it spray against her bedroom window and pound like pellets on the roof. Olivia hopped out of bed and made sure the chaplet was still on top of the dresser, where she had carefully placed it last night. Sure enough, it was still there, safe inside its box.

She brushed her teeth, washed her face, and put her uniform skirt on quickly as she bolted down the stairs. She couldn't wait to get to school. She was sure today would be different—a good day. A gloomy, rainy day made no difference. Even math couldn't bring her down today. She was sure that St. Thérèse would guide her through the ups and downs of her second day of fifth grade.

After another breakfast of oatmeal with brown sugar and raisins, Olivia's mom handed her a brown paper sack.

"Here's your lunch, Sugar. Now don't forget to check the school lost and found for your lunchbox."

"Um…sure, Mom," said Olivia as she stuffed the sack into her backpack. Where was the lost and found? Maybe it was by the front office. She'd check as soon as she got to school.

"Careful not to squish your sandwich!"

"Okay, Mom."

Olivia's mom switched Lucy from one hip to the other. "Have fun with your new friends Hayley and Sabrina."

"Sure, Mama," Olivia said as she struggled with the zipper on her raincoat.

"Gotta go!" And she ran outside to the garage where her dad was waiting to take her to school. Even the rain splashing against the windows of the car didn't bring her mood down. Today was going to be a great day! Her first day of following St. Thérèse's Little Way! And Olivia was sure that St. Thérèse was going to send her a rose any day now to let her know that she was taking her worries and concerns to God.

Olivia leaned back in her seat and watched the windshield wipers of Dad's car go back and forth, back and forth. She wondered where the rose would turn up, and when. She looked out the window at the dark, wet morning. *Not a rose in sight*, she thought. *But that's okay. I'm sure one will show up somewhere.*

Her dad was talking to her and she hadn't even heard him.

"Livvy? You awake, Hon?"

"Oh, sorry, Daddy. I was just thinking."

"A little nervous today?"

"No, not at all! Things are going to be good today." After all, today was a day about making things right—with everyone. And God gave her the chance right when she got to school.

She bumped right into Chad, who was holding the door open for the wet students coming into school.

"Oh, sorry, Chad, didn't see you," Olivia murmured, still ashamed of yesterday's events at lunch and on the playground. It still pained her to think of the hurt she had seen in his eyes as he had quietly walked away. Most of all, Olivia had remembered the confused and sad look he had given her.

But there was none of that look now as Chad continued to hold the door open for her to get out of the rain.

"S'okay," he said. "So, you decided to come back to St. Michael's, huh?"

Olivia managed a grin. "Yeah, well, I didn't have much of a choice, but it's a good school so far."

"Yeah, well, wait until you try the sloppy joes at lunch."

"I brought my lunch today," Olivia said with a shudder at the reminder of lunch. She knew there was no way Chad could know about how they all had made fun of him at lunch. He had been sitting far away and couldn't have heard, but she was still embarrassed. If he only knew…

"Well, then you're safe…for today!" he said good-naturedly.

Chad is in such a good mood, Olivia thought as she started to walk away. *He's being so nice to me. After all I did yesterday. He knows I am friends with people who make fun of him. I wonder what he thinks?*

But Chad just smiled and continued to hold the door open for the rest of the kids coming in out of the rain.

"Olivia?"

"Yes?"

"I'm sorry about yesterday."

Olivia stopped dead in her tracks in the middle of the hallway. What could he mean?

"About saying you talk funny," he explained to her confused expression. "I'm sorry I made fun of your Texan accent."

Olivia bit her lip. After all she had done to him, some even behind his back, he had thought to apologize for an innocent teasing remark. *She* was the one who was supposed to be apologizing, not *him*.

"It's okay," she said and turned around to face him, although she looked down at her feet. She felt horrible.

"My uncle lives in Texas. He gave me a Dallas Cowboys T-shirt one time. He says it's really nice down there. Y'all forgive me?" Chad joked.

Chad's not so bad, Olivia thought as she started to walk to the classroom. *We got off to a rocky start, but I can make it right.*

"Sure!" she called back over her shoulder with a faint smile.

Suddenly Olivia felt a familiar nudge, deep down inside.

You can do it, Olivia. A little thing with great love.

Olivia hesitated. She wasn't quite sure she could do this. She wanted so badly to apologize, but the words just didn't seem to want to come. How could she possibly apologize enough for what she had done? She remembered a quote from St. Thérèse that her grandma had told her, "*Jesus offers you the cross, a very heavy cross, and you are afraid of not being able to carry it without giving way. Why? Our Beloved Himself fell three times on the way to Calvary, and why should we not imitate Him?*"

"Chad?"

"Yeah?"

"Can you come here for a sec?" She wanted to talk to Chad without all of the kids who were coming inside hearing her. They moved over to an area by the teacher's lounge, where it was quiet and away from nosy ears. Olivia took a closer look at Chad and realized the girls were right; his clothes were old and worn. Instantly she felt ashamed for noticing that.

"I'm sorry, too. For bein' a big jerk yesterday!" Olivia said. The words came tumbling out of her mouth.

She softened her tone. "There's no excuse for what I did... your book is ruined. I feel terrible."

Chad looked a little bit uncomfortable. And surprised.

"Um..."

"I'm going to buy you a new copy," she promised. "I've got some allowance saved up. *The Life of the American Tree Frog*, right?"

"Aw, that's okay," he said.

"No, it's the only way I can make it up to you. If that's even possible."

"I'm used to it from those girls."

"Why don't you tell on them?"

"I used to, but it made the teasing worse from them, so I stopped telling. Sister Anne Marie would probably suspend them if I told her everything they did, but I don't want that, so I just ignore it."

"Why not get them suspended?"

"I don't know. No use doing that, I guess."

"How come they don't get caught?"

"They're sneaky. They wait until the teacher isn't looking, or is out of the room. They have their ways."

Olivia was dying to know something. She had fretted long and hard about it. "Chad, why didn't you tell on me yesterday?"

Chad shrugged his shoulders. "You're new. I didn't want to get you into trouble. Besides, sittin' in those blue chairs in Sister Anne Marie's office? Not too fun." He squished up his face. "Trust me, it's worse when she's 'disappointed in you' than when she's angry!"

Olivia could not believe it. She had laughed at him and destroyed his book. He didn't turn her in to the playground moms. He didn't even want revenge on Hayley and Sabrina.

This confused Olivia, but suddenly she was reminded of the story Grandma had told her about St. Thérèse taking the blame for someone else's misdeed in the convent. She could have easily gotten one of the other sisters into serious trouble, but, like Chad, she chose not to.

"Thanks."

"Why do you hang around them?" Chad asked in response.

Olivia couldn't say anything. He had a point. Surely at this school there were other girls, nice girls, to hang around with. She thought of Jenna. She even had something in common with her. But Olivia was afraid.

"The bell's gonna ring," Chad said in answer to her silence. "We'd better head down to the room or we're gonna catch it. I've already been tardy once this week, and it's only the second day of school! But thanks, Olivia."

Olivia and Chad walked down the hall together to Room 20.

Olivia took a deep breath. She had done her first little act of great love. It felt good!

Ten

*"I feel that my mission is about to begin—
to make others love God as I love Him."*
–St. Thérèse

"Tomorrow's supposed to be a nice fall day," Mr. Thomas remarked one Saturday evening in late September as the family sat in the family room reading and watching TV. "What do you say we all go to the apple orchard after church? You can invite your new friends Hayley and Sabrina."

Olivia looked up from a puzzle book she was working on. She'd never been apple picking before, and it sounded fun.

"Could I really ask them?" she said as she put her book down. "I wonder if they'd want to go."

"Oh, I am sure they would," said her mother. "It seems like the Michigan thing to do in the fall. Your dad grew up going apple picking every September."

"It's really fun," her dad said. "I know a place named Baker's Orchard, where you go on a hayride out to the orchard and pick your own apples. If we pick enough, we can bring them home to make applesauce and pies."

Olivia was excited. She went to the phone to call her friends right away, but then stopped herself. What if she called Chad and Jenna instead? Ideally, it would have been fun to ask all four of her friends. Maybe it was time for all of them to be friends together, not in separate groups, but she knew that it wasn't time, and that Chad might feel awkward considering everything that had happened so far. She also knew their minivan would not fit everyone. She was forced to make a decision.

Chad's phone rang for a long time before anyone picked up.

"Hello?" came a faint voice on the other end.

"Hello, this is Olivia Thomas. May I please speak to Chad?"

"Of course." A few moments went by before Chad came on the other line.

"Hi, Olivia."

"Hi, Chad. What are you doing?"

"Oh, just finishing up my essay for Monday. Did you finish yours?"

Olivia sighed. "No, not yet. I've got one more paragraph to write. At least it only has to be two pages."

"Yeah, but two pages is a lot for me. I'm terrible at writing," Chad acknowledged. "Last year we had to do a report on the Native Americans, and when I got it back, I got a C minus. I'll sure be glad when it's over. If I had known how report crazy Mrs. Wells was, I would've begged Sister Anne Marie to let me skip the fifth grade!"

Olivia laughed then. "Oh yeah, right! You're that smart, huh? To skip a grade?"

It was Chad's turn to laugh. "Yeah, I really am! I don't know why I'm stuck in the fifth grade with all of you people!"

"Well, I heard that Mr. Matthews has even worse projects in sixth grade," Olivia volunteered. "And that we have to dress up as a world explorer, costume and props and everything."

"Oh yeah, the dumb explorer project. Maybe I won't ask to skip a grade, then. But it'll be funny to see you and the rest of the girls dressed up as men. Maybe you can get a fake beard."

Olivia laughed. "No way! Maybe I'll get to be a woman explorer."

"Uh…Sorry to tell you this, Olivia, but there were no women explorers back then. They were all men. You know, De Soto, Champlain, Columbus."

"Oh come on, I know there were women on those boats. Didn't they have wives?"

"Yeah, there were all right, but unfortunately I think they were cooking and cleaning."

"Oh." Olivia was perturbed. That didn't seem very fair. "Well, I am sure on one of those expeditions, a woman got off the boat and started exploring," she retorted.

"Yeah, you're probably right," Chad said with a laugh. "Anyway, we'll get to visit the sixth graders when they do their presentations in the gym. How did you know about it?"

Olivia stopped. She felt strange bringing up their names. "Hayley and Sabrina."

Chad was silent for a moment, and Olivia could feel the fun leaving their conversation. "Oh. Yeah, I guess they would know."

"Anyway," Olivia rushed to put in, "the reason I'm calling is that tomorrow my parents are taking me to Baker's Orchard and they said I could bring some friends. Want to come?"

"Um…" Chad was hesitant. "I really can't."

"Oh. Why not?"

"I just…have to stay home, that's all."

Olivia was confused. Maybe he only liked to hang out with

boys, like Zach. Maybe he didn't want to hang out with girls. But she'd seen him with Jenna before.

"It sounds fun, though. Bring an apple for me on Monday."

"I...was going to ask you and Jenna," Olivia said.

"She told me she was going to Cleveland to visit her grandparents this weekend. She won't be back until Sunday night," he said.

So there went her plan to hang out with Jenna and Chad tomorrow.

"Okay, well, another time, then," she said.

"Sure."

Olivia heard a faint voice in the background calling for Chad.

"Thanks for asking, though. I should get going now," he said quickly. "See you on Monday."

"Sure, see you on Monday," Olivia repeated, and then hung up.

Well, there was always Hayley and Sabrina. It would be fun to go with them, too, right? After all, if she wanted to follow St. Thérèse's Little Way, she had to give them another chance.

What was it Grandma had said? St. Thérèse was all about love. Thérèse had made it her life's goal to love everyone, and to help them to love Jesus as much as she did. That seemed like a hard task to Olivia, but she could at least try. After all, Grandma had said that big or small, young or old, loving people was something anybody could do.

As it turned out, Hayley and Sabrina were more than happy to go.

"Your sister's so cute," Sabrina said when they were all piled in the minivan the next day. "Hi, little Lucy!"

Lucy responded by letting out a giant squeal.

"I think she likes you," Olivia told Sabrina.

"What about me?" Hayley wanted to know, and made a goofy face for Lucy's entertainment.

Lucy immediately started to cry.

"You scared her, Hayley!" Sabrina said in mock admonishment. "Aww, poor Lucy. Don't be scared of mean old Hayley."

"Babies don't like me," Hayley said flatly. "They always cry."

"Oh, that's not true, Hayley," Mrs. Thomas said from the front seat, a bemused look on her face. "Lucy, come on now, it's okay."

Lucy, strapped in her car seat, blubbered a little before settling down.

Olivia reached over and wiped the tears off Lucy's face with her hand. "It's okay, Lucy. These are my friends, Hayley and Sabrina."

Baker's Orchard was jammed. "Looks like everyone has the same idea," her dad remarked as he drove around the gravel parking lot, searching for a spot.

"We always go to Dixon's Orchard," Sabrina remarked. "They have pony rides and a haunted house on weekends."

Nobody said anything, then Sabrina hurriedly put in, "But Baker's is good, too."

"Kinda neat how the name is Baker's," Mr. Thomas said as he turned into a parking spot. "We're going to do a lot of baking with all of the apples we're going to pick, aren't we, Olivia?"

Olivia looked down at her feet. She was a little embarrassed that her dad had mentioned baking in front of Hayley and Sabrina.

"Sure, Dad."

Inside the big building, the smell of freshly fried doughnuts greeted them. Gallons of cold apple cider were for sale. Families were milling around, buying apple butter and caramel apples with nuts. Through a giant window, they could see doughnuts coming out of the fryer, soft and warm. Olivia's mouth started to water.

"We'll buy some of those on the way out," promised Mrs. Thomas. "Apple cider, too."

The straw on the hayride was itchy and poked Olivia through her clothes. They all sat on bales of hay as the man started up the tractor and pulled them all on a bumpy ride out into the orchard.

"The apples we're picking today at Baker's are Macintosh and JonaGolds," the man called out as he stopped the tractor in front of rows of trees. He handed out bags to everyone as they got off the hayride. "Have fun!"

There were rows and rows of trees just bulging with apples, as far as the eye could see. How did you choose a tree? Olivia couldn't wait to start picking.

"You girls can go over in that aisle if you want to," her dad directed. "I'm going to help Mom with Lucy's stroller."

The three girls giggled and chatted happily as they wandered over into the row of Macintosh trees. It was a beautiful fall day, sunny and cool. Perfect to be out with your friends and picking sweet, juicy apples.

"So what do we do?" Olivia asked Hayley.

"I don't know; I've never done this before," Hayley said, shaking her head.

Sabrina's head snapped back to Hayley. "What do you mean? You've been apple picking before, Hayley."

"No, I haven't."

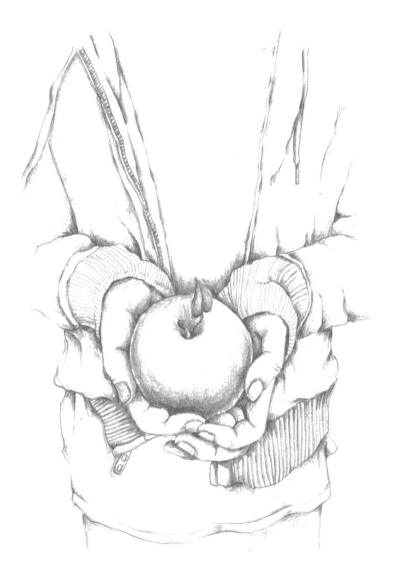

"Not even on field trips?"

"No," she said, growing a little impatient. "Nobody ever took me. It's no big deal."

"Oh," said Sabrina. "Well, there's nothing to it. You just find a tree you like, and pull an apple off. Nothing too complicated."

Olivia walked over to a tree and tugged at the first apple she saw. It was bruised and discolored.

"Don't just take the ones from the bottom branches," Sabrina said. "Look it over first before you pick it. And don't ever take the ones from the ground. They're rotting."

Sabrina, who was taller than the other two girls, proved to be quite helpful in reaching the upper branches.

Olivia reached for an apple and began to inspect it. To her horror, it had a small worm emerging from it.

"EEW!" she cried. "A worm!"

"It's no big deal," Hayley laughed. "I'm not afraid of bugs. Are you scared of a little baby worm?"

Olivia curled up her lip. She was not a fan of bugs or insects of any kind. They were creepy. She squished up her face as she held the apple in her hand. Then she slowly began to laugh.

"What?" Hayley asked.

"Oh, I was just thinking of a story my grandma told me about a saint who hated spiders," she said. "She couldn't stand them."

"Who was that?"

"St. Thérèse of Lisieux. She was this really great nun who lived in France in the 1800s. She was really sweet and loved Jesus a whole lot. She lived in a convent and one of her jobs was to clean the stairwells. She had to sweep under them with a broom and she was terrified of sweeping up spiders. I would be, too!"

Olivia then tensed, hoping that no one would make fun of her for bringing up her favorite saint.

"So what did she do?" Hayley wanted to know, looking genuinely interested.

"She did what she had to do," Olivia said, and shrugged her shoulders. "And she never complained about it. She tried to be really brave and pretended she was Joan of Arc going into battle with her sword."

Olivia looked down at the apple with the worm crawling out of it. She gently tossed it aside.

"You have to admit, he is kinda cute," Hayley said as she bent down to study the apple.

It didn't take long for the trio to have their bags bulging with freshly picked apples.

"I'm going to try one," said Olivia, who began to shine an apple on her shirt. She took a bite and her mouth instantly became alive with the juicy, tangy taste of an apple fresh from the tree. She had never tasted an apple so delicious.

"YUM," she cried. "Y'all, I never knew apples could taste like this!"

"They're always better fresh from the tree," Sabrina said knowingly as she took a bite of her own apple. "Mmmm...So much better than apples from the grocery store. They're all mealy."

Olivia soon realized what she had been missing in Texas. Apple juice dripping from her chin, she smiled and tossed the core to the ground. "Y'all, I think we need more bags!"

After everyone had picked enough apples, it was time to head back to the main building on the hayride. *This is so cool to be here at the apple orchard with my friends*, Olivia thought. They'd had such a fun time today. Nobody had teased or said anything mean about anybody else. Nobody argued.

Olivia looked across the trailer to Hayley and Sabrina, who were sitting opposite her, the late-afternoon sun shining brightly on them. Dad had been right; there was nothing quite like autumn in Michigan. She gave her friends a happy smile and they smiled back in return as they bumped along the dirt roads of the apple orchard.

Eleven

"There is only one thing to do here below: to love Jesus,
to win souls for Him so that He may be loved. Let us seize
with jealous care every least opportunity of self-sacrifice.
Let us refuse Him nothing—He does so want our love!"
—St. Thérèse

On the first of October, Grandma Rosemary stopped by after school with a surprise for Olivia.

Olivia was sitting on a blanket on the floor with Lucy, building a block tower for Lucy to knock down and laugh. They played this game over and over again while Lucy exploded into laughter. Olivia loved how Lucy laughed: a deep, gurgling belly laugh only a baby could have. When Grandma walked into the family room, Olivia leaped up and gave her a big hug.

"Grandma!"

"How's my Livvy doing today?" she asked.

"Great! I thought today was your day at the senior center."

"It is, but I'll go tomorrow instead. Today is a very special day, and I thought I'd come over to give you a little something."

She set down a pretty pink gift bag on the coffee table. "Open it," Grandma encouraged as she picked up Lucy from the blanket and gave her kisses on top of her head.

"I wonder what it could be?" Mrs. Thomas chimed in with a knowing smile on her face. Obviously, her mom was in on this too!

Olivia happily tore into the tissue paper and pulled out a beautiful white book entitled, *Reflections of St. Thérèse of the Child Jesus.*

It was a beautiful book with actual photographs and stories about the life of St. Thérèse. Olivia had never seen a real photo of her before, and she stared intently at a picture of St. Thérèse as a young girl with curly light brown hair in ringlets. Thérèse had been a gorgeous child, with a sweet, round face.

"She was adorable!" cried Olivia, pleased with her new present. "What a cute little girl." She flipped through the book and scanned the pages. It was filled with quotations of things St. Thérèse had written in the autobiography she had penned when she had become ill.

"Today is October 1st, St. Thérèse's feast day. It's her special day to be remembered," Grandma commented. "I saw that book at the Catholic bookstore and saved it for you until today."

"Thanks, Grandma." Olivia gave Grandma a big hug. "I can't wait to read it."

After Olivia finished her homework that night, she settled into a cozy chair in the family room to look through her new book about St. Thérèse. Most of the quotations were taken from the book she had written, *The Story of a Soul.* Others were taken from actual letters Thérèse had written to relatives and friends. Olivia found it fascinating. Some of the quotations were difficult for her to understand, but others seemed to leap right off the page. One story in particular seemed to speak to her:

> *My first victory was not a very big one, but it cost me a great deal: someone or other had left a little vase on a window sill, and it was found broken. Our Mistress thought it was my fault. She seemed very annoyed that I had left it there and told me to be more careful next time, adding that I had no idea at all of tidiness. Without saying a word, I kissed the ground and promised I would take more care in the future. Such little things, as I have said, cost me a great deal because I was so lacking in virtue, and I had to remind myself that it would all be made known on the Day of Judgment.*

Olivia was stunned. Imagine taking the blame for something you did not do. How difficult that would be! She shook her head. There was absolutely no way she would ever be able to do that. *Maybe I'm too prideful*, she thought, *but I would always want to stick up for myself. I'd never let anyone get away with doing something and let the blame fall on me!* Olivia didn't know that St. Thérèse had other plans.

Olivia managed to follow St. Thérèse's Little Way without anyone fully realizing what she was doing well into the end of October, when the leaves turned from green to gorgeous shades of crimson, orange, and yellow. Having lived all of her life in Texas, Olivia was astonished to see the trees come alive in such vibrant colors right in front of her very eyes. They were so much prettier in person than in pictures she had seen.

Their beauty seemed to inspire her to do even more kind acts. She raked the leaves when they fell without being asked. She kept an eye on Lucy when Mom was trying to cook dinner or take a phone call when she would rather have been reading alone up in her room.

She dusted the living room when Mom wasn't looking. She picked up Lucy's toys and put them away in the toy box. Olivia realized that she loved doing these things in secret, nobody seeing her. She realized that God would approve of her doing these things without making a big show of it. She remembered that in school last year on Ash Wednesday, her teacher had read a Scripture passage mentioning that very thing:

> Take care not to perform righteous deeds in order that people may see them; otherwise, you will have no recompense from your heavenly Father...And your Father, who sees in secret, will repay you. Matthew 6: 1, 4

Still, Olivia had to admit that she enjoyed seeing the puzzled looks on her parents' faces when they noticed that these little things had been done without prodding. If they asked, she would own up to what she had done. After all, it wouldn't be right to lie.

The Little Way was proving to be quite fun. One day she left a batch of raspberry white chocolate muffins she and her dad had baked on Sister Anne Marie's desk. She attached a note with a smiley face and nothing more.

Another day she straightened up the books in Mrs. Wells' independent reading area and shelved them nice and neat during indoor recess. When Mrs. Wells had come back, she was pleasantly surprised to see them so orderly.

When her spelling homework, although correct, looked a little sloppy, she reluctantly decided on her own to redo it so Mrs. Wells could read it easier. She printed extra neatly and had to laugh, because Grandma had told her that St. Thérèse was a terrible speller and struggled with that subject. She could relate, but for math.

Olivia figured that, as long as she was doing these little acts of kindness for God, she was helping to make the world a better place, one kind and loving act at a time.

It wasn't always easy. She wasn't always in the mood to do good things for people. Sometimes Olivia was in a bad mood, or tired, or swamped with a difficult math assignment when the opportunity to do a good deed arose. It was at those times when a little voice said to her, ***Olivia, ask yourself: "Am I pleasing my Jesus?"***

At St. Thérèse's gentle nudging, Olivia would stop what she was doing and do a little thing with great love, whatever it was that her heart advised her to do. She always felt better afterward. She never once regretted following St. Thérèse's Little Way.

Twelve

"Jesus, how tenderly and gently you lead my soul!"
—*St. Thérèse*

*I*n late October, the leaves on the trees in Olivia's back yard were on the ground, and the branches were barren. The Thomas family had raked all they could, but they had a lot of trees and the work soon got to be exhausting. Once in a while, Olivia would stop and lean on her rake, taking in the expansive back yard. She so wanted to explore, especially toward the back where there was a lot of growth. But she always found herself too tired from raking. Either that or it rained. It sure rained a lot in the fall in Michigan!

Olivia tried her hardest to help her mom and dad. She'd found a smaller rake in the garage among the garden tools the previous owners had left. Among them were trowels, shears, a digging tool, and a soil scoop. She took the rake and tried to rake in between the bushes, which proved to be difficult. The rake kept getting stuck in the bushes.

"Maybe next year we should hire some of the neighborhood boys to rake," Mrs. Thomas said with a yawn. "This is exhausting. I've never seen so many leaves!"

Olivia walked over to the edge of a huge pile, closed her eyes, and fell backward into it, laughing with delight as the soft leaves welcomed her fall. She'd never done this before, and it felt good. *Wait 'til I tell Claire and Emily*, she thought as she picked out the leaves that had clung to her long brown hair.

It was getting chilly outside, and eventually the family came in to enjoy bowls of homemade tomato soup for lunch. Grandma was slicing some fresh bread when they came in, all weary and tired, chilled to the bone from the cold October day.

"Wash your hands, everyone, and sit down. You must be starving!"

"Definitely!" said Olivia tiredly. She felt like she could collapse right there in the kitchen.

"I'm glad I'm too old for that and the neighbor boy Paul rakes my leaves," Grandma said. "Besides, I get to watch Lucy. I got the better end of the deal," she said, winking at Lucy, whose high chair tray was strewn with bits of bread and macaroni and cheese.

"I noticed the squirrels got to your pumpkins on the front porch," Grandma said, bringing a steaming bowl to the table and setting it in front of Olivia. "You're going to need a new one for Halloween."

It was true; the Thomas' front porch was a mess of chewed-up pumpkin parts. *The squirrels sure had their fill,* thought Olivia.

And soon Halloween would be here. It was coming up fast. She thought how fun it would be to go as a French chef. It had been Grandma's idea. Maybe she could even wear a mustache and a tall chef's hat, if she could find one. There was a cooking store in town; maybe they sold chef's hats.

Olivia wondered about her first Halloween in Michigan. Who would she go trick-or-treating with? What costumes were Hayley and Sabrina going to choose? They hadn't made up their minds yet. Jenna said she was going as a doctor. Her mother was going to let her wear the lab coat she wore to work at the hospital. But she said she always trick-or-treated with her cousins in their neighborhood, and was disappointed that she wouldn't be able to go with Olivia in hers.

When she asked Chad about his Halloween plans one day at recess, he seemed as if he didn't want to talk about it.

"Want to come trick-or-treating in my neighborhood?" Olivia asked as they played basketball. Chad was winning.

"I don't know," was all he said. "I usually don't go out."

"Why not?" Olivia asked, incredulous as she stopped dribbling and held the ball for a moment. Who didn't go trick-or-treating on Halloween? She didn't mean her comment to sound rude, but she was genuinely shocked.

From the sidelines, Jenna hurriedly put in, "It doesn't matter. We have a fun Halloween party at school. We have a costume parade and we play games and have popcorn and watch a movie."

By the look on Jenna's face, Olivia got the feeling she should stop asking questions. Sure enough, Jenna changed the subject to the upcoming social studies test.

Olivia got the hint. There was something about Chad that was different. He was funny and sarcastic and fun to be around, but when certain subjects came up, he seemed to shut down and get very uncomfortable. She was starting to realize that there were some subjects that were simply off limits with Chad. And that was okay. She just wished she knew what they were before she opened her big mouth. He was teased enough; she didn't want to embarrass him further.

One day, a few days before Halloween, when Sabrina started

to tease Chad at recess, Olivia told her to stop and leave him alone. She didn't use her temper. She was polite but firm.

"Y'all, that's enough now. I mean it."

Olivia was ready for anything—a teasing remark about her accent, or flat-out ignoring her demand. At first the girls raised an eyebrow at what she had said, but they seemed to forget it and got distracted by a game of tag that had started up.

"Come on, Hayley," Sabrina called. "They're playing tag."

Wow. That went over really well, Olivia thought. They didn't include her, but that was okay. Olivia shrugged her shoulders. Maybe this would be easier than she'd previously thought.

Olivia began to see her new mission was to protect Chad from the teasing. What was it St. Thérèse had said? "My vocation is love." Grandma had explained it by saying that a vocation is like a mission, something you feel called to do by God. St. Thérèse felt called by Jesus to love everyone to the best of her ability.

Could love be Olivia's vocation too? She could certainly try.

Thirteen

"Oh, how good a thing and how peaceable it is to be silent of others, nor to believe all that is said, nor easily to report what one has heard!"
—St. Thérèse

For a while, things seemed to be looking up in Olivia's life. She started to catch on to the math and she got an A on a test. The Thomas family had celebrated by going out for ice cream the night she brought it home. She'd stopped biting her nails, with the help of a terrible-tasting polish her mom had bought at the drugstore to stop nail biting. It seemed to do the trick. But best of all, there were times when Hayley and Sabrina could be nice. They complimented Olivia on her clay sculpture in art class. Hayley offered to read at school Mass, and Sabrina volunteered to help Sister Anne Marie with the baby blankets for the poor project after school.

Mrs. Wells' class was knee-deep into adding fractions when Sister Anne Marie knocked quietly on the classroom door. Immediately all pencils were put down. One thing all of the kids at St. Michael's knew was when the principal comes to your room, you stop whatever you are doing!

Olivia was relieved to have a needed break from fractions due to Sister Anne Marie's visit. How she hated math! It made her feel all frustrated and itchy.

Then she remembered how St. Thérèse learned to love suffering, teaching that it is the secret to piety. In the new book Grandma had given her, she had read a little story about a time in the convent when the sisters were praying together. St. Thérèse was trying to concentrate, but she kept getting distracted by the noise of another sister playing with her rosary beads. It really began to bother Thérèse and she began to sweat from the irritation of the jingling, clicking noise. She kept trying to ignore it, but finally she decided that she was thinking about it the wrong way. She wrote, "I set myself to listen as though it had been some delightful music, and my mediation…was passed in offering this music to our Lord."

Olivia sighed. Wouldn't it be wonderful if she could imitate this Little Way when it came to schoolwork too? She could sure try. She decided it would be beginning tonight, at homework time, which was her least favorite time of the day. She loved spending time with her father, but sitting at the kitchen table struggling to understand math concepts while he tutored her was not the way she wanted to do it. There would be eraser shavings all over the table and sometimes she'd end up crying out of frustration. Olivia would much rather have been playing a board game or baking sugar cookies with her dad.

But if she tried to think about it in a new way, like St. Thérèse had done, it might teach her patience. And she knew it would please Jesus if she worked on being patient.

"Hello, fifth graders," Sister Anne Marie smiled warmly. "I thought I would come to say hello. I don't mean to interrupt your lesson, Mrs. Wells."

Mrs. Wells stopped writing on the whiteboard and turned toward the door. Olivia thought she looked especially pretty today, in a red and blue floral skirt with a matching red sweater and a colorful beaded necklace. Mrs. Wells had the nicest clothes of any teacher she had ever seen.

"Oh, of course not. You are always welcome in Room 20, Sister Anne Marie. Class, let's greet Sister Anne Marie." Mrs. Wells capped her dry-erase marker and looked at the class expectantly.

At her prompting, the class said slowly in unison, "Good morning, Sister Anne Marie."

Sister Anne Marie, a loving but firm nun, nodded her approval. When she saw the math problems on the whiteboard, she said, "Ah, fractions. My favorite things! I remember teaching them when I was a teacher."

"When were *you* a teacher, Sister Anne Marie?" Chad asked, without raising his hand. "You're a nun!"

A small frown came over Mrs. Wells' pretty face and she looked disapprovingly at Chad. Chad turned red.

But Sister didn't seem to mind. "Oh, many moons ago, Chad. Long before you were born! I've been a principal for about thirty years. But math was my favorite subject to teach, especially fractions. I know Mrs. Wells is doing a wonderful job at it!"

Mrs. Wells beamed.

Olivia loved Sister Anne Marie from the start. She gave out the best hugs and always seemed to have a smile on her face. The kids respected her so much that they never wanted to disappoint her. She wasn't a yeller. In fact, no one ever remembered her having to raise her voice beyond an octave. But when Sister Anne Marie was mad, you knew it. The frown on her face spoke more volumes and was ten times more effective than shouting words ever could be. In most cases, the disappointment on Sister Anne Marie's face after a kid did something stupid was punishment enough. She just had a way of making the kids *want* to do the right thing. Teachers and students alike revered her. How could they not love a principal who told her children each day that she loved them before ending the daily announcements on the PA? A true blessing to St. Michael's, that's what Olivia's parents had said after meeting her.

Unfortunately, Olivia could not share Sister's enthusiasm for fractions, which tormented her every night at the kitchen table when her father helped her with her homework.

Sister Anne Marie turned to go. "I'll let you get back to your lesson now. Oh!" suddenly she remembered something.

"I have a few volunteers for the Peabody Center baby blanket drive, but I could use a few more. We have about a month to collect blankets. Anyone who is interested, have Mrs. Wells write your names down. We can use all of the hands we can get," she said. "Have a wonderful day!"

After Sister left, Mrs. Wells faced the class.

"Class, I strongly encourage everyone to consider donating new or gently used baby blankets for the Peabody Center, if you haven't done so already. Our goal is 150 blankets for underprivileged newborn babies who are poor. Sister didn't say how many we have already—"

Sabrina's hand shot up.

"Yes, Sabrina?"

"I'm helping Sister with the project," she said, "and yesterday we counted 78 blankets!"

She sat back in her chair, satisfied that she could provide Mrs. Wells with the answer.

"That's wonderful, Sabrina. Class, how many more do we need?"

More math. That was Mrs. Wells, always a teacher! Well, that was okay; Olivia thought she knew the answer.

Hands quickly shot up throughout the room.

Mrs. Wells scanned the room and settled on Olivia's.

"Sixty-two," Olivia answered confidently.

Hayley and Sabrina giggled softly.

Drat! Math was such a pain! She meant to say seventy-two. There was a little matter of ten.

After finishing the lesson, Mrs. Wells went to her desk and counted out some math review worksheets for the children to do quietly. Seatwork wasn't Olivia's favorite part of the day—far from it. As she reached for her pencil sharpener inside her desk, she felt something land in her hair and fall to the ground. Next to her shoe was a paper airplane. Making sure Mrs. Wells' back was turned, Olivia quickly picked it up and opened it.

Chad needs a haircut, don't ya think? Ha Ha! It's out of uniform. Hopefully he'll wind up in Sister Anne Marie's office! And I'll bet he forgot to bring his lunch again! What a weirdo! Write back!

Embarrassed, Olivia shoved the note inside her desk. She wished Hayley would stop writing her notes during class. Or was it Sabrina's handwriting? She couldn't tell. At lunch she was going to tell them to—

"And what do we have here, Miss Thomas?"

Olivia froze. She could see a pair of navy blue heels standing next to her desk. Slowly she lifted her head to see Mrs. Wells looking down on her, a frown on her face.

"Um…"

"Passing notes, I see?"

Olivia was silent. She didn't know what to say. This was the first time she had seen Mrs. Wells look mad. It surprised her, but then again, even the nicest teachers could get angry sometimes.

"No, not—"

"Perhaps you would like to share the note with the rest of the class, seeing as you couldn't wait until lunchtime to converse with your friends."

Olivia cleared her throat. "No, Mrs. Wells, that's really not necessary."

Mrs. Wells opened the lid of Olivia's desk and pulled out the wrinkled paper airplane. She briefly scanned the contents of the note.

"I see—a trajectory note to boot."

Mrs. Wells' good mood was gone. Long gone. Some of the kids looked over at Olivia, eyes raised. Nobody liked it when a kid spoiled the teacher's good mood. It ruined it for the rest of the class.

Trajectory. What did *that* mean?

"Mrs. Wells? What does trajectory mean?" asked Chad. Ugh, of all people to ask that! If he only knew the contents of the note...

Olivia squirmed in her seat. She couldn't help but think that Chad did not have very good timing for his scientific question. Sheesh.

Mrs. Wells didn't answer right away. She kept looking at Olivia. Disappointment was written all over her face.

As she answered Chad's question, Mrs. Wells kept staring at Olivia. "That's a very good question, Chad. It refers to something that is able to fly."

Mrs. Wells glanced toward the ceiling and sighed.

"I admire your interest in aerodynamics, Olivia, but note passing is not allowed in my classroom, especially airborne notes." She took the note back to her desk. "Class, resume your worksheets. Olivia, I want to see you in the hallway."

"Yes, Ma'am," Olivia answered sadly as she stood up and headed for the door. She glanced back at Sabrina. It must've been her who had written the note, because Sabrina mouthed the word "Sorry" to Olivia, and the strange thing was, she looked entirely sincere when she did it.

The class stirred, and she could hear them making nervous comments as she opened the door. Apparently Mrs. Wells never sent anyone out into the hallway. Until now.

She waited nervously in the hallway for Mrs. Wells to come out. This was absolutely terrible. What would Mrs. Wells say? What would her parents say? Would she have to go down to Sister Anne Marie's office to sit in the blue chairs? She dreaded that thought. She had never been sent down to the principal's office before, ever.

Her heart pounded. To pass the time and distract herself, she examined the writing projects her teacher had hung on the walls. The title of the project was, "A Saint to Me Is..." The class had chosen an important person in their lives and wrote about why that person was special to them. Most of the kids had chosen their moms or dads. Olivia had chosen Grandma Rosemary. She wrote what a wonderful role model and friend she had in her and how they had lots in common. She looked further down the wall. Olivia was surprised to see that Chad had written about his grandmother, too.

"My grandma is a saint to me," he'd written. "She teaches me right and wrong. She can't walk but she takes care of me the best she can every day."

Olivia wondered what that meant. Why was Chad's grandma taking care of him? Where were his parents?

The door to the classroom opened and Mrs. Wells came out, note in hand. Olivia stood up straight, waiting for her punishment, whatever it might be.

"You were right to say this note should not have been read aloud," Mrs. Wells said, her voice stern. Then it softened. "Olivia, I am surprised at you. This note is very cruel. Who wrote those things about Chad?"

Every fiber of her being wanted to tell Mrs. Wells the truth about who had written the awful note. Why let Sabrina get away with it? After all, she deserved to get into trouble for what she had done, didn't she?

It was at that moment that the voice of St. Thérèse spoke in her heart.

Follow my Little Way, Olivia. It will lead you to God.

And so it was that Olivia looked into Mrs. Wells' gentle brown eyes and said, a tear falling onto her cheek, "Mrs. Wells. I am so sorry, but I can't tell."

Mrs. Wells gave her a hug and held her for a bit.

"It's okay, Olivia. I know you are a good girl and don't want to betray a friend. I'm going to rip this note up and throw it away. Chad has not seen it, so no harm done there. I'm trusting you to tell whoever wrote this note how cruel it is."

"No more notes," she sniffed into Mrs. Wells' sweater. "I promise."

She had taken the rap for Sabrina, when all she had wanted to do was tell Mrs. Wells who had really done the bad thing.

It was a huge sacrifice, but she knew St. Thérèse was proud of her.

Fourteen

*"If heavenly grace and true charity come in,
there shall be no envy or narrowness of heart,
nor shall self-love keep its hold. For divine
charity overcomes all, and dilates all the
powers of the soul."*
—St. Thérèse

Soon it was time to wrap up the math lesson and get ready for lunch. What a morning it had been. Olivia slipped her hand inside her skirt pocket and fingered the dollar bill her mother had given her for lunch that day. Tacos, her favorite, were on the menu. That would definitely cheer her up. Her stomach growled. She wished Mrs. Wells would finish the math lesson so they could go to lunch. She wanted to forget the morning's incident with the note and start over fresh this afternoon.

Finally it was time to line up and head to the cafeteria. Hayley and Sabrina headed to their usual spot to sit down while Olivia waited in line, starving. She could smell the tacos coming out of the kitchen and her mouth started to water. She clutched her dollar bill and waited as patiently as she could. She glanced at all of the yummy-looking food on the lunch counter. Lunch ladies were

handing out plates of hot tacos, bags of chips, granola bars, and apple juice to the children who handed them their change.

She glanced at the wall next to the cash register where there were paper decorations of pumpkins and candy corns. A large posterboard hung beside them. She had never noticed it before, but then again, she didn't stand in the lunch line very often because her mother usually packed her a lunch. The poster listed names of kids who owed the lunch ladies for peanut butter and jelly sandwiches. Olivia had never had a school PB&J before. It was mostly for kids who forgot their lunches at home. They were supposed to pay the lunch ladies when they could, and then their name would be crossed off the list. Most of the names she didn't recognize, except one that stood out: Chad O'Toole.

Suddenly, Olivia felt that familiar feeling she was beginning to know all too well.

Pay for Chad's sandwich. It is in giving that you shall receive.

Olivia bit her lip. The sign said that school sandwiches were 75 cents. If she paid for Chad's sandwich, that would mean she'd only have a quarter left for her own lunch today. And a quarter could only buy...she looked at the counter.

A bag of pretzels was a quarter. A crispy rice treat was a quarter. That wouldn't be that nutritious, though. Her mother wouldn't approve of that. A banana or an apple was a quarter. She could have a PB&J herself and pay tomorrow, but she was allergic to peanuts so that wouldn't do. And a jelly sandwich didn't sound appetizing. What she really wanted were tacos. A girl in front of her paid for her taco lunch and walked away to her table. They smelled so good! Her stomach growled again. Surely there would really be no reason to—

"Yes, Honey?" asked the lunch lady, somewhat impatiently. Olivia's turn was up.

"What can I get you?"

"I...uh..." Why was this so hard today, to follow the Little Way?

"Sweetie, we don't have much time and the line is long. What can I get you?" the lunch lady repeated.

"Um...this is for Chad O'Toole's peanut butter and jelly sandwich." She held out the dollar. "And for a quarter I'd like a banana, please."

"Sure," the lunch lady said as she grabbed a banana out of the bowl for her and took her dollar. "Is that all you want?"

"Yes, ma'am," Olivia answered softly.

The lunch lady studied Olivia's face. "Is the rest of your lunch at the table?"

"Yes, ma'am," she said. After all, she got a carton of milk every day and her mother had prepaid for that. Milk and a banana were a nutritious lunch, even if it was small.

As Olivia walked away toward the milk bin, she saw the lunch lady take a big black marker and cross Chad's name off of the sandwich list. A warm feeling grew inside of her.

"Is that all you're eating?" Hayley eyed her banana when Olivia sat down. She shoved a handful of cheese curls into her mouth and her teeth turned orange.

"Yeah, I'm really not all that hungry today," Olivia said as she unpeeled her banana. And, strangely enough, she really wasn't anymore.

Fifteen

"I realized that all souls have more or less the same battles to fight, but no two souls are exactly the same."
—St. Thérèse

"Olivia, Honey, at least have one more bite," Olivia's mom urged her as she poked at her pizza.

"It's your favorite, mushrooms and pineapple," Grandma said encouragingly. She was staying for dinner and was going to help her mom and Lucy hand out candy to the trick-or-treaters who were soon to arrive.

Normally, Olivia would have eaten two slices, but she was way too excited to eat. It was Halloween night, after all. A night to have fun and forget about the bad grade she had just gotten on her math test. A night to forget about her problems, dress up, and get candy.

The sky was getting darker and darker and she couldn't wait to get into her costume to go trick-or-treating. Hayley and Sabrina were due at her house any minute, and they were all going to get dressed into their costumes when they arrived.

"Okay," she relented, and took a couple more bites to please her mom and grandma.

"ACHOO!" her dad sneezed loudly, making everyone jump. Her dad was such a loud sneezer. It always drew attention, especially in public, which ashamed Olivia to think it, but sometimes it embarrassed her.

"God bless you, Dad," said Olivia. "Are you sure you're okay to take me trick-or-treating?" Her dad had an awfully bad cold.

"Thanks. Well," he sighed. "I don't see that there's much choice, Honey. Mom, Grandma, and Lucy are handing out candy and Mom has to put Lucy down to bed soon. Heaven knows she never goes to sleep for me," he winked at Lucy.

"You really don't look good, Steven," her mom told her dad. "I think maybe I'll be the one to take Livvy out tonight."

"I'll be fine," her dad said. And sneezed again. "It's Livvy's first time trick-or-treating here."

Olivia beamed. She couldn't wait to go trick-or-treating for the first time in her new neighborhood. The only downside was when her mom told her that she'd have to wear a coat over her chef costume.

"A coat? We never had to wear coats in Texas on Halloween," Olivia complained.

"It was never 40 degrees on Halloween night, Livvy," her grandma reminded her. "You'd freeze without a coat."

Olivia sighed. She wouldn't look very authentic with her big puffy parka over her white chef's coat. How silly she would look, with a big chef's hat on her head and a big pink parka!

"The other girls will have coats on too," her mom said. "It'll be good to see Hayley and Sabrina again."

Olivia took her plate and glass to the sink. Her mom did not know most of the things Hayley and Sabrina said and did at school, mostly because Olivia kept hoping they would improve their behavior. She'd been asking St. Thérèse as part of her Little Way to help the girls shed their nasty ways. So far, Olivia had not seen them reform. Come to think of it, her math grades were still pretty dismal too. It was tough not to get discouraged, but Olivia felt like St. Thérèse was still watching over her, even though she hadn't seen much improvement in her daily life, nor seen a rose. As Grandma had said, it takes time. She knew she should be patient and give St. Thérèse time to work.

The doorbell rang, breaking up her thoughts.

"They're here!" she cried happily and ran out of the kitchen to answer the front door.

She swung the door wide open, revealing two fairy princesses and a ghost, only about three feet high.

"Trick or treat!" they shouted with glee.

Olivia, disappointed that it wasn't her friends, smiled and reached for some mini chocolate bars to toss into their bags.

"Y'all look great," she told them and their faces lit up. "Happy Halloween!"

"Thanks, you too!" yelled the kids as they ran off the front porch in search of more candy at a neighbor's house.

Olivia shivered and went to close the door. It really was chilly out tonight.

"Boo!" shouted a loud voice as someone jumped out from behind the big maple tree in Olivia's front yard!

Olivia looked up with a start. Hayley!

She laughed loudly. "I sure scared you!"

Hayley had on a girl rock star outfit, complete with an over-the-ear microphone, a pink wig, and a plastic electric guitar. She held out a leg to show off her white leather boots. "Cool, huh? My mom got me this costume off the Internet."

Olivia thought her costume was really cool. She looked very grown-up. She noticed that Hayley wasn't wearing a coat, only a long-sleeved shirt.

"Aren't you cold? My grandma says I have to wear a coat," Olivia groaned as she invited her inside.

"Ugh! A coat would ruin the look," Hayley said with a wince. "Here in Michigan we layer under the costumes so it doesn't look so bad. My brother forced me to at least wear these long sleeves. Do you think rock stars wear long sleeves? I don't think so!"

Olivia laughed. "Come on in. Where's your mom?"

"Oh, she had to work late. My brother Ryan drove me over; he's waiting outside on the sidewalk. He's going to go along with us instead if that's okay."

"Sure. I just have to get my costume on. Where's Sabrina? I thought she was coming with you."

"Me too," said Hayley as the two walked into the kitchen. "But she called me at the last minute and said that she's running a fever. Her mom gave her some Tylenol and she's stuck home in bed."

Olivia was sorry to hear that, but something deep inside her was glad, too. Not for Sabrina's misfortune, of course. She would never have wished illness upon anyone. But going trick-or-treating alone with Hayley sounded fun. She never got to hang around with Hayley alone; Sabrina was always around. It might be a good way to really get to know the real Hayley. Olivia guessed that Hayley might be a different person if she didn't have to impress Sabrina.

Luckily, once Olivia had told them not to write her any more notes in school, the two girls had complied. After all, they told her, it was never their intention to get her into trouble.

"She can have some of my candy," Olivia offered. "It always ends up going stale because I can't eat it all. Too much makes me sick anyway."

Hayley paused. "That's really nice of you, Olivia. You know, Sabrina still feels bad about getting you into trouble with that note."

"It's all over with," Olivia said. "I really don't want to talk about it anymore. Let's just forget it ever happened."

"Well, hello there, Hayley. It's good to see you again," Olivia's mom said as she came to greet Hayley, breaking up the awkward conversation.

"Hi, Mrs. Thomas. Thanks again for taking me to the apple orchard. I had fun."

"Of course. Over there is Olivia's grandma, and you remember Mr. Thomas, and little Lucy."

Hayley was afraid to make too much of a fuss over Lucy, seeing as she made her cry last time.

But Mrs. Thomas' warm southern accent had made her feel comfortable instantly, just like it did the first time.

"Hi Hayley," said Olivia's dad. "I wouldn't come too close to me or I'll sneeze your wig right off!"

Hayley laughed.

Grandma waved. "Hi there, Hayley!"

"ACHOO!" her dad sneezed. And then, "ACHOO!"

"Well, if you two want to go upstairs and finish getting ready, Olivia can lead the way," her mom said pleasantly. "I'll come up with some hot cocoa and cookies in a few minutes."

Olivia has such a nice mom and dad, Hayley thought. Somehow she couldn't picture her mom making hot cocoa for her friends. But she worked all of the time. It wasn't her fault that

Dad had died when she was seven, leaving her and Ryan to fend for themselves a lot after school.

The two went upstairs to Olivia's room and shut the door. Hayley looked around the room, giving it a once-over.

"Nice room."

"Thanks."

"You sure have a lot of stuffed animals," she said as she flopped on her bed.

Olivia felt a little embarrassed, thinking maybe her room was a little babyish. She had never felt self-conscious about her belongings until now. Back in Texas, her friends all had the same kinds of toys and decorations in their rooms. But things were different here with these girls. She was living in a new state with new friends who had new interests. She wondered what Hayley's room looked like. She hadn't been invited to her house yet.

Hayley dug into her trick-or-treat bag and pulled out a little zippered case.

"I need a mirror for my makeup," she announced.

Olivia handed her a small hand mirror she kept on her dresser.

"Makeup?"

"Sure, I'm a rock star, aren't I? I need to do my face to complete the look," she said with a slightly exasperated tone as she adjusted her wig. "This is itchy."

She unzipped the bag and produced two eyeliner pencils, a blush compact, and a tube of lip gloss.

Olivia bit her lip.

"Your mom lets you wear makeup in fifth grade?"

"Of course not, silly. But Ryan doesn't care, and he won't tell," she said as she pulled her lower eyelid down to apply a thick line of black liner.

"I swiped this from my mom's drawer. She won't notice it's gone tonight and I'll put it back right when I get home."

Hayley. *I guess she is the same—whether she's around Sabrina or not,* Olivia decided sadly. Oh well. Hayley's bad behavior was not going to ruin her fun tonight. That was her problem to deal with when she got home, not hers.

"Your mom will see your face all made up," Olivia pointed out, trying to be helpful. She didn't want Hayley to get into trouble when she got home.

Hayley rolled her eyes, exasperated with Olivia. "Olivia,

don't be such a goody two-shoes. Anyway, take a look at this," she said. She held up a travel-sized makeup wipe package. "I'll just wipe it off before I go inside."

"Okay, well, I guess I'll change into some long-sleeved shirts and a jacket before I put my costume on," Olivia said as she headed to her closet and yanked some shirts off of hangers.

"By the way, what are you going as?" Hayley asked.

"A French chef," Olivia answered. "Can I borrow your brown eyeliner to make a mustache?"

Hayley handed her the eye pencil. "I guess so. But don't ruin it, or my mom will know."

"Okay, thanks."

Olivia grabbed an armload of clothes and left the room. "I'll be right back."

"Take your time, I'm still doing my makeup," Hayley announced. "But I need some tissues. I made a smudge on my left eye."

Olivia pointed to her nightstand. "There's a box there."

"Thanks."

The door closed and Hayley was left alone in the room. She got up from the bed and looked around. It was a large room, much larger than her own. In fact, Olivia's whole house was much bigger and prettier than hers. She suddenly felt very jealous.

What a babyish room, she thought. Stuffed animals and Pioneer Girl dolls, even a couple of old Care Bears. Hayley giggled softly to herself. Olivia was such a good girl. She liked her, but sometimes it drove her and Sabrina crazy.

Suddenly she had an idea.

A very funny idea.

She'd show Olivia how to have a little fun tonight. She grinned at the thought of it. But how to make it work with Mr. Thomas and Ryan trick-or-treating with them? That was the problem.

She went back to studying Olivia's room. The bed had a beautiful floral comforter with pink and purple flowers and matching pillowcases. It looked brand new.

There was a cherry wood desk with matching bookcase containing rows of books and a set of purple floral bookends. A white wicker basket overflowed with coloring books and stickers. Another held Pioneer Girl dolls and piles of doll clothes that spilled out over the carpet.

A half-finished latch-hook rug of a brown pair of kittens lay on the floor with stray bits of yarn. A laundry basket was filled with uniform skirts waiting to be put away. For being such a goody-goody, Olivia sure had a messy room. A happy feeling welled up inside Hayley. So, Miss Perfect wasn't so perfect after all. It wasn't much, but it was something.

A beautiful white crucifix hung over her bed. Hayley felt a twinge of guilt as she glanced at it, knowing what she was planning for that evening.

She shook her pink head to rid herself of the guilt and went about looking for a tissue. On the nightstand, Hayley found plenty to nose through. A *Little House on the Prairie* book, a picture of a pretty saint in a clear plastic frame. Who was that? She turned the frame over and read "My sister in Heaven, St. Thérèse of Lisieux."

Puzzled, Hayley put the picture down. Sister in Heaven? But Olivia only had one sister: Lucy. She didn't get this. It was in Olivia's handwriting, but it made no sense. Whatever! Olivia *was* a little strange sometimes.

Next to the picture was what looked like a pretty bracelet with pink rose beads all over it and a small medal. It looked like a mini rosary. Hayley picked it up and felt the beads. It was pretty. She didn't own anything like this. She studied it more closely. The picture on the medal resembled the pretty picture in the frame. *This must have something to do with this saint*, she thought.

She rubbed the beads between her fingers. *What a lucky girl to have such nice things*, Hayley thought.

Suddenly, the urge was too much. She slipped the chaplet under her costume into her pants pocket.

A knock on the door made her jump.

The door opened slowly and Mrs. Thomas came in holding a tray with two mugs and a plate of cookies.

"I know y'all will be having plenty of sugar tonight, but what's cocoa without cookies, right?" Mrs. Thomas said. "I sure hope your mom doesn't mind."

"Oh no, she doesn't care," Hayley said quickly. Her mom cared, of course, but certainly not about something as insignificant as this.

Mrs. Thomas cleared some papers off of Olivia's desk and set the tray down.

"Have you ever seen such a messy room? This weekend, Olivia is going to clean it up and we're going to donate some of these extra things to St. Vincent de Paul. There are so many people in need," she said with a sigh.

She looked a little closer at Hayley. "I see you've done your makeup."

"Yeah. Well, I have to look...authentic," Hayley said.

"Oh, that's true, and it is Halloween after all," Mrs. Thomas agreed. "Olivia's in there doing a French mustache, which we'll never get off in time for school tomorrow, she's putting it on so thick!"

"Oh, she can use these," Hayley said helpfully as she held up the makeup remover wipes.

Mrs. Thomas smiled at Hayley. "I'd appreciate that, Hayley. Thanks. Can I give you a tip?"

"Sure, Mrs. Thomas."

"Your makeup's a little heavy. Even for a rock star as cool as you," she said. "Mind if I help a little?"

Hayley shook her head. "Nope."

"Well," Mrs. Thomas said, taking a wipe out of the pack, "I know a little about makeup, and in every situation, the *natural* look is best, even for a Halloween costume."

She wiped Hayley's left eye, then her right. She took a fresh wipe and wiped dark streaks of pink blush off of Hayley's face.

"Now, I am not condoning your wearing makeup. Don't misunderstand me. You are way too young to be even thinking about wearing it, but since it's Halloween and part of a fancy costume, I suppose it would be okay. Let's start from scratch. This eyeliner pencil is pretty dark, so a soft line is best, see?" She took the pencil and dabbed faintly along each eyelid.

"There. Now, a little blush for color, just like this," and she brushed a very faint blob of color on each cheek and blended it in with her fingertips.

"And just a little dab of this," she said as she opened the lip gloss tube and lightly applied it onto Hayley's lips. "Rub your lips together."

Hayley did as she was told and looked into the handheld mirror. She liked what she saw. Before, she had looked like a clown. Now she looked nicely dressed up in her costume.

"The key is *tasteful*," Olivia's mom said gently. "Just so it's barely there. You want to be wearing the makeup, not the makeup to be wearing you," she said. "And when you're much older and ready to wear makeup, when you're *grown up*," she said pointedly, "you'll know just what to do." She winked at her.

Hayley felt a warm feeling inside her. Olivia's mom was so kind and loving. Her mom could be like that, too, if she could be around more and had the time. Things were just so harried at home with only one parent and her mom working full time.

"Have you ever worn makeup before? I know you aren't allowed to at school, of course, but have you worn it when your mom isn't around?" Mrs. Thomas raised an eyebrow.

Hayley looked down. She really didn't want to lie, but she didn't want to tell Olivia's mom that she sometimes sneaked behind her mom's back when she wasn't around.

Mrs. Thomas patted her on the back. "It's okay. I'm not going to yell at you or tell your mom or anything. But you should know something, Hayley. When young girls your age do things that adult ladies do, like wear makeup, sometimes other people don't realize that they're only eleven years old. They might expect you to act older than you are."

"What's wrong with acting mature?" Hayley wanted to know.

"Mature is one thing, if it means acting like a lady. Being polite and respectful and modest. But young girls with makeup don't look mature, they look…well, silly. It isn't a very wholesome, tasteful look at your age. Don't try to grow up too fast, Honey. Once childhood is gone, it's gone. You will have plenty of time to be a grown-up lady who can wear lipstick."

She patted the wig on Hayley's head. "I know I just met you. I don't mean to be your mom or anything. I guess I just can't turn off my mommy mode. That's what happens when you become a mom. But you look tasteful and nice in your costume now. Don't ya think?"

Hayley nodded, but she was embarrassed that Mrs. Thomas had seen her looking so ridiculous earlier. In fact, she felt really dumb.

"I think Olivia's almost done and then you girls can start out. I'll grab a lightweight fleece of Olivia's for you to wear under your costume. It's cold out there. See you downstairs," her mom said with a wink and left the room.

Hayley went over to the desk, picked up a mug of cocoa and took a sip. So what if she had embarrassed herself? Mrs. Thomas was nice and what she said sort of made sense.

Pangs of jealousy entered Hayley's heart. Olivia sure was lucky to have a mom like that, who knew important things about growing up. It was almost like she could read her mind. Maybe her own mom would talk to her like this, if she had the opportunity.

Olivia was also lucky to have a room like this. *Too* lucky.

She shook her head. Should she put the pretty bracelet back? Should she continue with her plan for tonight? She couldn't decide. Sometimes she felt like a nice girl, who worked hard in school, was helpful around the house, a good friend. Other times she felt angry and jealous, spiteful and mean. Why was she so divided?

Just then, Olivia entered the room, clad in a white chef's jacket and a tall chef's hat. She had a funny brown mustache drawn over her lip.

"Ta da! How do I look?"

"Great. You look like a real chef," said Hayley, suddenly getting impatient. She wanted to leave this room. "If we don't leave now all that will be left will be dental floss and raisins. Ready to go?"

"Sure, but guess what? My dad is just too sick to go," said Olivia, looking anxious. "He mentioned that maybe your brother could take us instead. Think he would mind?"

This was too perfect.

"No, not at all," Hayley said with a slow grin, thinking of how that would make tonight's plan that much easier.

Sixteen

"What a trial! But He whose Heart is ever watchful taught me that He works miracles even for those whose faith is like a tiny mustard seed, to make it grow, while, as in the case of His Mother, He works miracles for His dearest friends only after He has tested their faith...this is how her Beloved dealt with His Thérèse—a long testing, and then He realized all her dreams."
—St. Thérèse

Hayley and Olivia went up and down Olivia's block, their bags so full of candy that they could barely carry them.

"Sabrina hates coconut, so don't give her the Mounds bars," Hayley told Olivia, who had started to dig through her bag on the way back to her house. Ryan walked behind them with flashlights.

"I like trick-or-treating on your street. It's more fun than mine," said Hayley as she struggled with her heavy bag.

"Where do you live?" asked Olivia, wishing she could eat a mini Hershey bar. Her parents insisted on checking the candy out before she ate any.

"Oh, not too far from here," she said vaguely.

"Are there many houses on your street you go to?"

"Nah. Not many."

Olivia didn't know what to say to that.

"I have an idea," Hayley said, "A really cool one."

Olivia was curious. "What?"

"Wait a minute." Hayley dropped her bag on the sidewalk and ran back to Ryan. She whispered something to him that Olivia couldn't hear. Then he shrugged his shoulders and said, "Sure, why not?"

Hayley ran back to Olivia. "We've got more houses to do. Go empty your bag at home and let's ask your mom if we can go over to another street."

Olivia was unsure. She wanted to, but it was getting late—and cold. The wind was picking up, too, lifting her chef's hat off her head. She had to chase it down the sidewalk a couple of times.

They also had school tomorrow. And her legs were getting pretty tired from walking around all night.

Hayley saw her hesitation and rolled her eyes.

She didn't want to disappoint Hayley, though. And who could say no to more candy?

"Oh, come on," she said impatiently, and pulled on Olivia's arm, dragging her up the front walk of her house.

Mrs. Thomas and her grandma were handing out candy to a bunch of middle-schoolers when they walked up.

"Hi girls! Did y'all have fun? Looks like you got a lot of candy tonight. Why don't you both come inside and I'll check it over for you two?"

"Well, Mrs. Thomas, we were wondering...Since Sabrina is sick, I told her I'd give her some candy, and we need to go get some more."

Mrs. Thomas eyed their bulging candy bags.

"You've got quite a stash there. I'm sure between the two of you, you'll have plenty to give her."

"I know, but I thought we could go to a few houses on Sabrina's street and then stop by her house to give her some. Would it be okay if my brother took us there really quick? We'll come back in a half hour, I promise."

Mrs. Thomas looked at Olivia's rosy cheeks and pleading face. "Please, Mama. It would be fun to stay out an extra half hour. Please?"

At that point Ryan walked up the walk. "It's really no trouble, Mrs. Thomas. I'll bring her right back."

Mrs. Thomas was undecided.

"I'll stay right with them."

Mrs. Thomas was quiet for a minute, then said, "Well, it's only 7:30. I guess it's okay if you come home in a half hour. There's school tomorrow."

"Thanks Mrs. Thomas!" yelled Hayley as she pulled Olivia's hand again and they ran to her brother's car.

"Thanks Mama!" yelled back Olivia.

"Not too long!" yelled Mrs. Thomas after the girls.

"I thought you said Sabrina lives way past the mall," Olivia asked Hayley as they piled into the back seat of Ryan's old car. "We'll probably be longer than a half hour."

"Nah, where we're going won't take long. There's one house I want you to see," she said.

Seventeen

"The Lord is a rock upon which I stand; He teaches my hands to fight and my fingers to war. He is my protector and I have hoped in Him."
—St. Thérèse

Olivia was happy to be out so late on a school night, having fun with Hayley. Normally she'd be at home getting ready for bed about this time. She felt very grown-up being in the back of a teenager's car with Hayley, driving around in the dark. Ryan took a corner quickly, causing her bag of candy to tip over, spilling much of its contents.

"Slow down a little, Ryan! Sheesh!" yelled Hayley to her older brother as she bent down to retrieve Olivia's candy for her.

"Sorry, girls. I wanted to make the light."

Ryan fiddled with the radio as he drove, finally settling on a station that played rock music. A song came on that he liked, and he started to sing along and tap his fingers against the steering wheel. Olivia thought he looked silly, getting so into the song, and she laughed. It wasn't a song she particularly liked, but watching Ryan goof off was entertaining. He looked over his shoulder and yelled out over the music.

"Too loud for ya back there? I can turn it down."

"No, not really," Olivia said, wishing he would so she and

Hayley could talk. She guessed that was what older teenaged brothers did, play music loud and drive fast.

Olivia turned to Hayley and whispered loudly in her ear over the music.

"You're brother's nice, Hayley."

"Yeah, he's pretty cool," she agreed. "A little too overprotective sometimes. He watches me a lot when my mom's at work."

The car turned onto Binson Road, a street with smaller homes mixed in with old apartment houses, some badly in need of repair. The street wasn't as bright as Olivia's. Some of the street lights were out and only a few porch lights were lit. Ryan's car slowed down and parked in the street in front of a red-brick apartment house. Olivia started to get a bad feeling. She didn't see any kids trick-or-treating, either. It is getting kind of late though, she reasoned. Most of the kids had probably gone in already. They were starting to dwindle on her street, too.

"The sign says Binson Road. I thought you said the name of Sabrina's street was Chestnut," Olivia asked.

"It is."

"Then why are we parking here? Hayley, this isn't Sabrina's street."

Olivia leaned into the front seat to speak to Ryan.

"Ryan, where are we?"

Ryan had his music playing so loud that she had to repeat her question.

"Hey Ryan! Where ARE we?"

"My sister said you wanted to visit a friend from school first before going to Sabrina's," he said, confused. "Isn't this the place?"

"Yeah, it sure is! Come on, Olivia. " She nudged her out of the car and onto the grass.

Ryan rolled down the window. "Hey!" he shouted. "You two left your candy bags in the car!"

Hayley ignored her brother and pulled Olivia behind a huge oak tree. "We'll be right back, Ryan!"

Ryan sighed. "Whatever." He turned down the music, took out his cell phone and dialed a number so he could pass the time while he waited for Hayley and her friend. The things he had to do for his goofy sister sometimes! Fifth-grade girls could be so strange.

"Why aren't we going to Sabrina's street?" Olivia demanded.

"Sshh! Keep your voice low!" Hayley let out a soft giggle. "Forget Sabrina. See that apartment house in front of us? See the window on the second floor?"

Olivia felt silly and a little scared standing under a big tree at night in a strange neighborhood. The wind whipped around her as they huddled under the tree, cutting through her layers of clothing under her costume. Suddenly she felt very cold. Her teeth started to chatter.

"Hayley, I—"

"That's Chad's house!" she giggled again. "Or old, dingy apartment, I should say. That's his room!"

"Chad? But...why are we at Chad's?"

"I just wanted to show you where he lives. Weird, isn't it?"

Hayley fished around in her pocket and produced a small handful of hard butterscotch candies, which she began to pelt, one by one, in the direction of Chad's window.

"What are you doing?" cried Olivia in shock.

"You don't think I'd waste the Snickers, do you?" Hayley whispered between throws, which thankfully were poor ones.

"Hayley, STOP IT," Olivia said frantically, her voice getting louder. She tried to grab her arm, but Hayley moved it away too quickly and Olivia missed.

Hayley laughed wickedly and held up a piece of candy.

"Wake up, Chad! Trick or treat!" she yelled as her last piece of candy hit Chad's window with a loud ping.

"Bullseye!" she shouted and exploded into laughter, pleased with herself.

A chill rushed down Olivia's spine, and it wasn't from the brisk, windy night. She absolutely could not believe what Hayley was doing. Her fists clenched and teeth gritted, she turned to Hayley in the moonlight and stared at her. Never in her life had she felt so disgusted.

"You are the most stuck-up, mean person I have ever met in my life. I don't even know why I am friends with you, Hayley. I want to go home RIGHT NOW! I hate you!" Her temper was at the boiling point.

With that, she turned and stomped back to the car in the darkness.

"Wait!" yelled Hayley loudly, who had forgotten to whisper. "I'm sorry! Olivia, don't be mad!"

Olivia ignored her and kept on walking. She was pretty sure that this is not what St. Thérèse would have done in this situation, but she knew she had to get away from Hayley at that moment.

"Olivia! I said WAIT UP!" she yelled at Olivia's back as Olivia picked up her pace to run to the car. A strong gust of wind made her fall over onto the dark grass. As she scrambled to get back up, the wind lifted her chef's hat off her head and carried it away in Hayley's direction. She didn't care. With her long hair whipping around her face in all directions, she kept moving. She just wanted to get in the car and go home.

"Take me back home, Ryan. I want to go home NOW!" she barked at Ryan once she was back in the car.

"I thought you two wanted to visit a friend," he said.

"That's what I thought too. But it turns out that HAYLEY is no friend of mine!" she shouted, her temper getting the better of her. She couldn't help it. She hated Hayley!

"OLIVIA!" shouted Hayley across the lawn as she ran back

to the car. "I said I was SORRY!" She got in the backseat and slammed the door shut.

Ryan put the car in gear and drove off noisily down Binson Road.

Up on the second floor, a curtain in the window quickly drew closed. Inside, Chad turned off the light and got back into bed.

Eighteen

"I'm certain of this—that if my conscience were burdened with all the sins it's possible to commit, I would still go and throw myself into our Lord's arms, my heart all broken up with contrition; I know what tenderness He has for any prodigal child of His that comes back to Him."
—St. Thérèse

Hi St. Thérèse. This was the worst Halloween in history. Well, at least *my* history. I'm sure you saw what happened tonight. It was awful, just awful. We were having such a good time trick-or-treating and then Hayley lied to me. She had us go over to see where Chad lives so she could make fun of it. Who does she think she is? She always thinks she is better than everyone else. Oh, I really, really hope Chad didn't see us. He would feel terrible, even worse than I do right now.

St. Thérèse, I don't know what to do anymore. You haven't sent me a rose yet. I've looked everywhere. Are you too busy to hear me? I don't mean to be disrespectful, but things are getting harder, not easier. Math is getting harder, the girls seem to be getting meaner. I've tried to make friends with other girls in class, and they are nice enough, but they all have their own friends. Maybe they are afraid to be friends with me because I hang around with Hayley and Sabrina. Maybe they think I am like them. I've tried to be nice to everyone, including Hayley and Sabrina, but following your Little Way is really hard for me.

I didn't tell Mom and Dad about going to Chad's. I didn't want them to get Hayley in trouble and make things even worse for me, even though Hayley deserves to get into trouble for what she did tonight. I can't believe I told her I hated her. I've never said that to anyone before.

St. Thérèse, please continue to pray for me. And please send me a rose so I know you are listening.

Good night.

Olivia closed her eyes and tried to get comfortable in bed, but she was too upset. The whole evening had been ruined by Hayley's antics. She tossed her panda bear Fuzzy aside and folded her arms across her chest, dejected.

Do not be discouraged.

Olivia's eyes flew open. Where did that come from?

Confidence is the weapon to fight discouragement.

Olivia clutched Fuzzy to her chest. St. Thérèse was guiding her again. She was telling her not to give up, to keep praying and trying her best. To stick with the Little Way to please Jesus and not give up, even when you wanted to and things were hard and you got so mad at people you could scream.

Olivia wondered if St. Thérèse ever got mad at people, like she was now. Grandma had told her a story of an unfriendly sister in the convent with her who did everything she could to annoy Thérèse. Some of the nuns even stayed away from this crabby nun, but not Thérèse. She forced herself to befriend her and spend time with her. One day the sister asked Thérèse, "Why do you spend time with me?" Thérèse had answered, "Because I like to be around you."

The truth was, she really didn't like to be around this nun, but she knew this nun needed her friendship, and she knew that God would be pleased with her efforts to befriend her. This began to soften the irritable nun and she became easier to be around.

Maybe Hayley and Sabrina were like that unfriendly nun. Maybe they needed Olivia's friendship even though she acted terrible sometimes. Jesus had always taught to pray for your enemies. Hayley felt like an enemy at the moment. She wasn't sure if she could forgive her. Then she remembered how Chad had forgiven her when she destroyed his favorite book. She guessed forgiveness worked both ways. "As we forgive those who trespass against us…" said the Lord's Prayer. Sister Anne Marie had said it was the most beautiful prayer ever written.

She closed her eyes. It would be tough, but she'd do it. She'd do it for Jesus, and she'd do it for St. Thérèse.

> Even though I'm REALLY mad at her, I'd like to pray for Hayley, St. Thérèse. Please ask God to watch over her and help her to be good. Help her to know that Jesus loves her.

It didn't take long for Olivia to fall fast asleep.

Nineteen

"Our Lord needs from us neither great deeds nor profound thoughts. Neither intelligence nor talents. He cherishes simplicity."
—St. Thérèse

Hayley wasn't at school the next day. With Sabrina still sick at home, Olivia found herself with no one to talk to at school, so she just sat at her desk that morning, waiting for the first bell to ring.

She lifted the lid of her desk and looked at the mess inside. *I guess now's a good time to clean some of this stuff out,* she thought. She picked out some stubby pencils and broken crayons and set those on her lap. Next she found a cracked ruler and some old tissues. Lastly, she pulled out an empty potato chip bag. She stuffed all of the garbage into the chip bag and walked it over to the trash bin. Then she sat back down to rearrange the notebooks.

What a slob I am, she thought. *If Mom could see this desk!* Then she remembered her messy room at home. She really ought to do a better job with that, too. She lost her St. Thérèse chaplet again and had spent a good part of the morning before school looking for it. This time it wasn't under the covers. It sure would make it easier on Mom if she didn't have to nag her as much. St. Thérèse would like that. Olivia suddenly remembered a story she'd read in one of Grandma's books about how Thérèse was not very good at housekeeping chores and would get in trouble for that in the convent. Olivia had to giggle as she thought of her bedroom at home and her school desk. She and Thérèse sure seemed to have a lot in common!

"Looks better. I should do mine," said a voice behind her. Jenna was peering into her desk looking admiringly at the neatly stacked books and folders.

"Hi, Jenna."

"Did you go trick-or-treating last night?" Jenna wanted to know.

"Sure."

"Yeah, me too. I went with my cousin Leah and her friends. They gave me all their Skittles."

"That's great."

"Skittles? Who said Skittles?" asked Chad, his eyes wide as he approached his desk and stuffed some crumpled homework pages inside. "I'll take 'em!"

"I've got about twenty mini bags of them," said Jenna. "I'll bring you some tomorrow. My mom won't let me eat them all anyway, not with these new braces." Jenna frowned. Of all the luck, having new braces on Halloween!

"Where are Hayley and Sabrina? Usually you're talking with *them* before school," Jenna asked, eyebrows raised.

"They're sick today, I guess," Olivia said.

"Were they sick last night too? Bummer," said Jenna. Did Olivia detect a bit of sarcasm from Jenna?

Olivia glanced at Chad, wondering if he had seen them last night. She turned red just thinking of standing under his window with Hayley laughing at Chad's home and pelting candy at his window. Suddenly she felt the butterflies come again. She had yelled at Hayley so loudly that he must have heard the commotion outside.

I should have known Hayley would have been up to some-thing, Olivia chastised herself. *When will I ever learn?*

But Chad showed no sign of emotion, or that he had seen anything last night.

"Sabrina was, but Hayley wasn't. So we went out trick-or-treating around my house," Olivia said vaguely. "She must have woken up with a cold or something." Olivia wanted to drop the subject. She had no idea why Hayley wasn't there today. *She had seemed healthy enough last night*, she thought wryly. *A little too healthy for her own good.*

Then Olivia caught herself. If you've decided to truly forgive someone, you don't think negatively about that person.

"Anyway, I hope she feels better," said Olivia.

"Yeah," Chad agreed, not the least bit sarcastic. Olivia took that to mean Chad had not seen them.

"Then why don't we eat lunch together today?" asked Jenna. "You can sit with Alexa, Zach, and me. You too, Chad."

Olivia felt a warm glow come over her. It was really nice of Jenna to invite her and Chad to join her friends.

The bell rang and Jenna skipped back to her seat in the first row. Mrs. Wells was eager to start morning prayer and announcements.

"Morning, everyone. I hope everyone had a fun and safe Halloween. Did you get lots of candy?"

The class nodded and several shouts of "Yeah!" could be heard. Olivia couldn't help but notice that Chad had stayed quiet. Maybe he didn't go trick-or-treating last night.

"Today is a very special day. Who can tell me what it is?"

Mrs. Wells, dressed in a pretty orange floral skirt and matching sweater, glanced around the room as she decided whom to call upon. Her gaze rested on Olivia.

"Olivia? What is so special about today?"

Olivia was glad she knew the answer. "It's All Saints' Day."

"That's right. Today is the day we honor all of the saints in Heaven. Does anyone have a favorite saint? I have one," she said with a smile. "It's Mary, the mother of Jesus. And so I especially love our special statue of Mary here in our classroom."

At lunch that afternoon, Olivia sat sandwiched between Chad and Jenna across from Alexa LaPointe and Zach Seever.

Chad opened a brown paper lunch bag and produced a sandwich, which he started to devour. It smelled like tuna fish.

"Ew! I hate tuna fish!" exclaimed Zach as he unwrapped his peanut butter sandwich. "It's stinky."

Olivia laughed. People, she found, either loved tuna fish or hated tuna fish. There was no in between.

"Peanut butter is even smellier," Chad jabbed back, but he wasn't mad, and took an even bigger bite of his sandwich.

"My grandpa made the best tuna fish sandwiches," Olivia said, feeling a twinge of sadness. "He died a few years ago. That smell reminds me of him."

Chad looked at Olivia's fallen face. "Sorry about that," he said.

"Nah, that's okay. I just haven't eaten tuna fish since Grandpa died. None of us have."

"My grandma always says death is nothing to be afraid of or sad about," Chad said somberly. "Her favorite saint got really sick and one of the last things she said before she died was, 'I am entering into life.' I bet things are a lot better on the other side, don't you?"

There was silence at the table. Sometimes Chad said things that were funny. Other times he said things that sounded grown up. Nobody knew what to say, except Olivia, who was curious.

"What saint was that?"

"St. Thérèse of Lis…Lis…something or other."

"Omigosh!" Olivia piped up. "Lisieux! She's my favorite saint, too. I'm going to do my saint report on her."

"I'm doing mine on St. Francis of Assisi," Chad said. "He liked animals. I bet he'd like Jumper."

Olivia wasn't paying much attention to what they were saying. She was too happily surprised to find out the coincidence of Chad quoting from St. Thérèse.

"I think I'll do mine on St. Anne, the mother of Mary," Jenna said thoughtfully. "You never hear that much about her."

"I don't know who I'm doing mine on," said Zach. "Chad, are you almost done with that tuna fish?"

Jenna unwrapped a plastic box with pasta salad inside. "My grandpa taught me how to make homemade bread," she said as she stabbed a forkful. "That is the best smell in the world."

"I make homemade bread with my dad," said Olivia. "He taught me how to bake when I was really little. We make it on weekends because it has to rise overnight. My mom says it smells like a bakery!"

Jenna laughed. "I know. My grandpa died too, so my mom and I do lots of baking now. Last weekend we made scones with cinnamon chips. They were sooo good!"

"I'd LOVE to learn how to make scones," Olivia said. "Yum!"

She dug in her lunchbox and found a mini Milky Way bar that she didn't want.

"Look what my mom put in. Who wants it?"

"I'll take it," said Chad. "Thanks, Olivia."

"Wanna come over after school today and bake something?" asked Jenna as she opened her milk carton. "All of you guys."

"Can't," said Alexa as she rolled her eyes at Zach. "It's Friday…we both have piano lessons. Ugh."

Olivia had always wanted to take piano lessons, but after listening to Alexa and Zach moan and groan about scales and practice books, she decided she wasn't so sure.

"I'll ask my mom when she picks me up from school today. Maybe she can drive me over if your mom says it's okay?"

"Sure."

"Chad?" asked Olivia. "Can you come?"

"Not today," said Chad quietly, concentrating on his sandwich.

"Oh, that's right," Jenna said quickly. "Another time, though, Chad, okay?"

Chad didn't answer and continued to eat his sandwich. Olivia wondered what had just happened. She felt like she was missing something. It wasn't like Chad to be so quiet.

The bell rang, signaling that it was time to clean up and head outside for recess.

"Why can't Chad come over today?" Olivia asked Jenna when Chad was out of earshot.

Jenna looked around to make sure they were alone as they walked toward their coat hooks.

"Grab your jacket and I'll tell you outside," she said. This was all too mysterious. Olivia got the feeling it was something important.

"Don't let this get around, okay?" said Jenna once the two were alone, which wasn't easy with the entire fifth grade out on the playground. They stood by the tether ball pole, which was not being used.

Olivia nodded, feeling very serious. Jenna took the ball in her hands and started to twirl it around the pole.

"You're nice, and I think I can trust you with this. Chad lives with his grandparents, and his grandma's kinda sick," Jenna said matter-of-factly. "Not too many people know it, just his good friends and Mrs. Wells and the principal."

"Oh. What happened to his parents?"

"They died a long time ago in a car accident when he was really little. He's lived with his grandparents ever since. They're really nice; I've met them before." Jenna twirled the ball all the way and then started to slowly unwind it.

Olivia thought back to their conversation at lunch and felt sad for Chad. He knew about losing a loved one; he had lost his own parents. No wonder he had seemed so serious when the topic had come up.

"His grandpa takes care of his grandma during the day, and after school Chad stays with her so his grandpa can go to work for a few hours. He bags groceries at the grocery store. They don't have much money."

Olivia thought of Chad's faded uniform pants and scuffed-up shoes. Hayley and Sabrina had made fun of his clothes. She wondered if they knew the true story. They couldn't have. They couldn't be that mean.

She also remembered their conversation just before Halloween when Chad said he couldn't go trick-or-treating. It was all starting to make sense now. He had to stay home to keep his grandma company while his grandpa worked.

"Are you sure nobody else knows?" asked Olivia.

"Yeah, pretty much. He keeps it to himself. He tries to hide it. He's not ashamed or anything, he just doesn't want everyone to feel sorry for him. But he likes you, so I don't think he'd mind. I feel pretty dumb asking him about coming over. Once in a while he can come, but he usually can't. I just forgot."

"Chad has to know that you didn't mean anything by it," Olivia tried to encourage Jenna.

"Yeah, he's really nice. He's kind of...different. Sometimes he can be really goofy and stuff and likes to be around people, and other times he likes to be serious and alone, like at lunch or recess. But he's such a great person, you know? He'd do anything for anyone. And he's super funny. Chad was really nice to me when I moved here and didn't know anyone. He introduced me to Alexa and Zach," Jenna said.

Olivia wondered something. Was Chad's grandma teaching him about the Little Way? She thought back to how he liked to hold the door open for the students in the morning, without being asked to. And how he had said he wouldn't turn Hayley and Sabrina in to Sister Anne Marie or Mrs. Wells. It was certainly possible.

"Is his grandma going to die?" asked Olivia. She thought of Grandma Rosemary and how terrible she would feel if something was seriously wrong with her.

Jenna thought about that for a second before answering. "I don't think so, not soon anyway. She just needs a lot help getting around and needs someone to stay with her in case she needs something. Chad keeps her company after school on weekdays."

"I promise not to breathe a word," whispered Olivia.

"Good."

"Hey!" yelled Chad, running up to the pole, out of breath. "Hogging the tether ball or what?"

Olivia smiled and unwound the ball the rest of the way. She tossed it over to Chad.

"Chad and I play first!" Olivia said.

Twenty

"The smallest actions done for His love are those
which charm His Heart."
—St. Thérèse

"Don't eat all the cinnamon chips," said Jenna, pretending to be stern. Olivia giggled and popped a few into her mouth and let them melt. "Mmmmm. Okay. Where do we start?"

Jenna slipped an apron over her head.

"Well, my mom preheated the oven, so let's start mixing."

"Wait, I know y'all have made these a billion times, but I haven't. First let's read through the recipe one more time to make sure we know what we're doing," said Olivia as she washed her hands in the kitchen sink.

That's what she and her dad did before starting any recipe. One time they forgot and realized halfway through a bread recipe that it was supposed to rise overnight. That had turned out to be a disappointment because they were forced to wait until the next morning to proceed with the recipe.

Jenna handed her a spotted recipe card that was well worn from years of baking the cinnamony treats.

The two girls had a good time mixing and kneading the dough

with their hands, the best way to incorporate all of the ingredients. Flour and sugar were all over the counter and Olivia accidentally got some eggshell in the batter, which she gingerly picked out.

They told jokes and laughed at tales Olivia told about Lucy's funny antics. Olivia found that she was really clicking with Jenna. They had so much in common. She hated to think it, but she was glad both Hayley and Sabrina were absent on the same day. It gave her a chance to meet a new friend. She probably wouldn't have had the opportunity to really get to know Jenna if Hayley or Sabrina had been at school that day. And she certainly wouldn't be here making scones in Jenna's kitchen.

Jenna's mom slid the cookie sheets of cinnamon triangles into the oven. Soon the warm, sweet smell of cinnamon drifted through Jenna's house.

"Smells heavenly," she said. "Save one for me!" She went to the stove and put the tea kettle on. "I simply can't have a scone without a spot of tea, my fine ladies," she said with a fake English accent.

Olivia giggled as Jenna poured them each a glass of cold milk.

"Yes, my dahling, but I prefer a glass of milk!" Jenna said, her nose in the air.

The scones were warm and buttery and tasted as good as they smelled. Olivia couldn't wait to copy down the recipe so she and Dad could make them sometime themselves.

Olivia was very proud of herself. She'd never tackled scones before, and they came out as delicious as she had hoped.

Their tummies satisfied, the girls went upstairs to Jenna's room to play while the rest of the scones cooled.

The first thing Olivia noticed was a big box filled with Pioneer Girl dolls and clothes.

"Hey, I like those too!"

"Then we're the only ones," said Jenna, picking one up and brushing its long blonde hair. "I bet Hayley and Sabrina don't play with them."

Olivia frowned. "Probably not." Suddenly she had a thought. "Hey Jenna, do you think we could all play sometime?"

"Who?"

"All of us: you know, Hayley, Sabrina, Chad, Zach, Alexa."

Jenna looked confused. "Why?"

"I don't know; it might be nice to all hang out together."

"Olivia, I don't think so. I hate to burst your bubble, but I don't think that mix would work. Besides, Chad is not going to play with Pioneer Girls. Neither will Zach."

Olivia laughed. "No, not dolls, silly. But just...I don't know, maybe going to a movie or something. Or playing at my house."

"You can't mix certain people together," Jenna said. "And I really doubt that Chad would even want to play with Hayley and Sabrina, especially because they treat him so badly."

Olivia had to agree. Her idea didn't sound so good anymore. But it was too bad.

The girls talked and played for a bit more until the doorbell rang and Olivia's dad came inside to pick her up. Jenna presented her with plastic zipper bags filled to the tops with the scones.

"These are for you!"

"For me? All of them? But don't you want to keep some?"

"Nah, that's okay. We make them all the time here, especially in the fall. You can take them home to your family."

Olivia, knowing there were way too many treats for her family to eat, paused.

St. Thérèse's Little Way came to mind.

"There's plenty to share with everyone else, that's for sure."

She thanked Jenna and her mom for a fun evening and walked out with her dad to the car.

"Have a fun time?"

"A fantastic time!" she breathed. "Dad? Mind if we drop some of these bags off to some friends?"

"I don't see why not. Where to first?"

"Do you know where Binson Street is?"

Twenty-One

"Love proves itself by deeds, so how am I to show my love? Great deeds are forbidden me. The only way I can prove my love is by scattering flowers and these flowers are every little sacrifice, every glance and word, and the doing of the least actions for love."
—St. Thérèse

A light was lit in the big front window of Chad's building, illuminating the darkness surrounding it. Olivia and her dad parked the car in the street.

"I won't be long, Dad," said Olivia. "I just want to give one of these bags to Chad."

"Want me to come with you?"

"Nah, that's okay. I know Mom's got dinner almost ready. I'll just stay on the porch."

She grabbed a zipper bag full of scones and skipped to the darkened porch to ring the bell. It felt strange to be on Chad's front porch when, just last night, she'd been hiding behind a big tree in the front yard. She shuddered with guilt at the memory.

A few seconds later, the front porch light flicked on. The door slowly opened ajar to reveal a little gray-haired woman in a wheelchair.

"Well, hello there, young lady," she said.

"Hello ma'am, my name is Olivia and I'm friends with Chad."

Olivia felt funny saying that. Was Chad really her friend now? Was it okay to say that she was his friend after all she had done?

"It's nice to meet you," she said sweetly. "Would you like to come in?"

"No thank you, my father's waiting for me in the car. I just wanted to drop off some cinnamon scones that Jenna and I made tonight."

Chad's grandma smiled. "Well aren't you the sweetest? I don't think I've met you before, but maybe I have. My memory isn't the greatest these days."

"Um, no, we haven't met yet," said Olivia. "I'm new to St. Michael's. My family recently moved here from Texas."

"Ah yes, the Texan girl," his grandma said. "I know Chad has mentioned *you*."

Olivia felt herself redden. Instinctively she felt the urge to bite her nails, but she forced herself to resist it. She wondered exactly what Chad had mentioned about her to his grandma.

As if to answer her question, his grandma took ahold of her hand and patted it gently.

"I'm so glad he's made a new friend."

Olivia heard the sound of a microwave beeping.

"Dinner's ready, Grandma," announced Chad in a cheerful voice, coming out from the kitchen. "Nothin' like exciting, left-over meatloaf—oh. I didn't hear the doorbell." He stopped and stared at Olivia. "Hi Olivia."

"Hi Chad." Awkwardly she thrust the bag of scones at him. "Jenna and I made these. Hope you like cinnamon."

"Thank you so much, sweetheart," his grandma said as she started to wheel away from the door. "Here Chad, I'll take these into the kitchen and we can have them for dessert when Grandpa gets home from work." She wheeled into the kitchen with the bag on her lap, leaving Chad and Olivia standing in the doorway.

As she watched his grandma leave, Olivia got a glimpse of the living room. It was sparsely decorated, with threadbare furniture and a small potted plant on a stand. She could see Chad's textbooks and a notebook laid out on an old coffee table. Chad followed her gaze into the living room but said nothing.

"Doin' your homework on a Friday night?" Olivia tried to lighten the mood. "I always wait and leave mine 'til Sunday night, but my mom and dad say that's not too smart."

"Yeah, and it's always my luck that I forget to do something and get a dumb 'missing assignment' from Mrs. Wells! So I started doing it early on weekends just in case," Chad explained. "See, I'm almost done and now I can relax and watch TV the whole weekend while you're slaving away!"

"Ha, ha," Olivia put in sarcastically.

It was quiet for a few moments. Olivia didn't know what to say, and Chad seemed to be lost in thought.

"Want to come in? You could meet Jumper."

"Oh no, thanks. I've got to get home for dinner. Although my stomach's full of these," she said, lifting the bags of scones.

"Yeah, sure, you're just scared of a tiny tree frog."

"Oh, sure!"

"Yeah, I think you are. I think you're scared of bugs and insects and stuff," Chad teased.

"I am not!"

"Then prove it. Wait there a minute."

Olivia waited awkwardly on Chad's front porch. He returned from the other room carrying a small plastic cage.

"Look under the grass. See him?" Chad asked proudly.

Olivia took a deep breath and bent down to peer inside. "I

don't see him," she said with relief that she tried to hide. She didn't want Chad to know that he was absolutely right about her being squeamish.

"He's in there. He's hiding. Come on out, Jumper," he coaxed.

Olivia bent down again to look inside the cage, just to appease Chad. Suddenly, the tiny tree frog jumped out from under the grass and plastered himself on the wall of the cage.

"Yikes!" Olivia recoiled. That thing had scared the living daylights out of her.

Chad threw his head back and laughed.

"Oh, come on, he won't hurt you, will you, Jumper?"

Olivia shivered. "He's…really cute, Chad," she said, trying to be nice. "Just don't take him out of the cage."

Chad laughed again and agreed.

"Okay. That was really nice of you to come over," he said. "My grandpa loves anything with cinnamon. So do I. There might not be any left by the time he gets home!"

"It's no problem. I'm off to deliver these to Hayley and Sabrina," she said, immediately feeling bad for mentioning them in front of Chad. "You know, since they've been sick and all."

Chad shrugged his shoulders. "Sure."

"I think Sabrina lives kind of far away so I'll have to drive over to her house tomorrow." Olivia felt like she was rambling, but she continued. "And I forgot that I don't know where Hayley lives, so I probably won't make it over to her house tonight, either."

Chad frowned. "No, you can deliver Hayley's tonight," he said, confused.

"Hmm?"

Chad poked his head out the front door and pointed.

"Yeah, she lives just down the street here."

Twenty-Two

*"I understand clearly that through love alone
can we become pleasing to God, and my sole
ambition is to acquire it."*
—St. Thérèse

Olivia could not believe it. Hayley lived on the same street as Chad. In the same type of home: an old apartment house, just like the one she had taken Olivia to see on Halloween night. To make fun of.

Olivia sat in the bathtub that evening mulling it over as she absentmindedly played with the bubbles she'd poured in. Why on earth would Hayley make fun of her own home? She just didn't understand. Would Sabrina have done the same thing if she were with them? She wondered.

Olivia had been to Sabrina's house, on a Saturday with Hayley to play, and had been immediately impressed by how new and fancy it was. Olivia had never been to a house that had twelve-foot ceilings and a kitchen so large that you could fit two of hers inside it. Sabrina's bedroom was huge, too, and filled with every toy imaginable. Olivia wondered what she did with all of her things when Christmas and birthdays came. But despite the fact that Sabrina was obviously a wealthy girl, she never really seemed to brag about it, for which Olivia was grateful. Even though Olivia's family was very comfortable and she had a nice house, she never really gave it too much thought what other people had. It wasn't important to her at all. She had just figured Hayley had a rich family as well, judging by the way she had acted on Halloween night. She was so confused.

After Chad had told her where Hayley lived, Olivia had mumbled a quick "thanks" and went back to the car. She didn't know why, but she had felt the strong need to go straight home instead.

She'd given Chad the other bags of scones. Maybe his grandpa could bring them over to Hayley's. She didn't want to embarrass Hayley by bringing them to her herself. Hayley obviously didn't want Olivia to know where she lived. *That must be why she hasn't invited me over yet*, she mused. It was so strange. In making fun of Chad's house, Hayley was actually making fun of her own.

Why would Hayley do that? Olivia didn't see what was so wrong about living on Chad and Hayley's block. So things were smaller and older; who cared? Olivia personally didn't care where her friends lived. They could live in a mansion or a small apartment; she didn't care a bit. All she cared about was having nice friends to play with and talk to. Olivia herself had grown up in a tiny house in Houston and had shared a bedroom with Lucy. Her friend Claire lived in a new house with five bedrooms in a fancy neighborhood. Nobody seemed to care, and that was the way it should be.

I wonder: if Hayley had seen my old house in Texas, would she have treated me any differently? What if she had seen my little bedroom that I shared with Lucy?

Olivia used the pink plastic cup she kept in the bathtub to rinse the fruity shampoo from her hair. The warm water she poured over her head was soothing and calming.

Dripping wet in her towel, she went to her room to change and thought about how her chaplet was still missing. She felt awful about it. If she didn't find it soon, she'd have to fess up and tell Mom and Dad.

She really needed to talk to St. Thérèse. She'd know what to do.

She combed out her wet hair and sat down on the edge of her bed.

> Hi St. Thérèse. As you can see, I am really confused. So many crazy things have been happening. I have been looking for a rose, St. Thérèse, to let me know that things will turn out fine at this new school with these new friends. I haven't gotten one yet. Maybe you are busy helping other people who need your help more. That must be it. I am trying really hard to follow your Little Way. I know I have to be patient, but it's really hard, Thérèse.

After she was finished praying to Thérèse, she sent up a silent prayer to God as well, asking Him to please listen to St. Thérèse if she decided to talk to Him on her behalf. She also asked Him to please bless all of her new friends at school.

A while later, in her cozy pajamas and slippers, she padded downstairs to work on her math homework with her dad. Like Chad had said, best to get it over with early in the weekend.

"All fresh and clean?" her dad asked her as she sat down at the table.

"Mmm hmmm," she said reluctantly as she took a newly sharpened pencil from her dad.

Olivia sighed.

Subtracting fractions.

It was going to be a long evening.

Twenty-Three

"The only happiness here below is to strive to be always content with what Jesus gives us."
—St. Thérèse

Dear Olivia,

It's Claire and Emily! We wanted to write you a letter together to say hi!

How is Michigan? How is your new school? Things are the same back here in Houston. We bet it is cold up there. Have you seen snow yet? Maybe it's too early. You have to make a snowman and take a picture of it. Send it to us and we'll bring it to school to show everyone! You are so lucky!

Cool news: We just signed up for a knitting class. It sounds fun! Lauren McKinley is going to be in it, too. Hey, maybe we can knit you some scarves to keep you warm up there in the winter. They might not turn out that great, though!

Guess what? Travis got sent to the principal's office last week for pulling Claire's hair in gym class. (And it really hurt!!) He had to apologize with an essay and everything. Same old Travis.

You are not missing anything. Any kids like him at your new school? We hope not!

We miss you! Let us know if you are coming back for a visit!

Love,

Claire and Emily

Olivia folded up the letter and put it back into the envelope. Claire and Emily had also enclosed a picture of them on Halloween. Olivia held it up to study it closely. Olivia felt sad looking at their smiling faces, suddenly missing them terribly. The two girls were arm in arm in front of Claire's front porch. Claire was dressed as the Statue of Liberty and Emily was dressed as a giant M & M. Olivia recognized it as the same costume Emily wore last year, when they had all gone out trick-or-treating. They'd had such a fun time, the three of them.

Olivia felt a twinge of jealousy. She wondered if they had new private jokes between them, like the ones they used to have together. They certainly had new experiences to talk about, ones she could not be a part of, like Travis getting into trouble or their new knitting class, which sounded exciting. Olivia had always wanted to learn how to knit. It would have been so much fun to learn to knit with them. She imagined Claire and Emily laughing as they struggled to learn the stitches together with Lauren McKinley. She frowned. It hurt her feelings to imagine them having fun together without her. But it wasn't Claire and Emily's fault that she had to move all the way up to Michigan.

Boy, if Dad hadn't gotten this new job, we could still be living in Texas. I wouldn't have all of these problems with Hayley and

Sabrina. I'd be at the craft store buying knitting needles and yarn with Claire and Emily.

Suddenly, Olivia's jealousy turned to anger. Why did things have to change? Everything was fine back home. Now she was living in a strange place with strange new people. And the rose she had been praying for was yet to show up.

Then it hit her: if she were still living in Texas, she wouldn't be able to see Grandma as much. That was definitely something great about leaving her old home.

She put the envelope in her top desk drawer, stuffing it among old postcards and drawings, crayons, and pencils. There was no way the girls could have known that their letter would make her blue, she reasoned. They were great friends, just trying to be nice.

She couldn't let her sadness and bitterness take over. She wondered, *What would St. Thérèse have done?* Then it came to her. She would've brushed away the jealousy and written them a nice letter, wishing them well in their new adventures and cheerfully telling them all about her new home. Olivia decided that she'd write them back that evening. After all, her homework was done!

"Olivia!" her mom called from downstairs. "Are you ready to go shopping now?"

The thought of going to the mall to buy new winter coats for her and Lucy did not excite Olivia, but she knew it had to be done. A northern winter was coming, and they had to be prepared for it. That meant new parkas, snow pants, and warm boots. Claire and Emily thought she was so lucky to be anticipating a true winter with snow. Maybe it was high time she started to appreciate these changes in the seasons. She knew that was what St. Thérèse would have done. She would have tried her best to be content, no matter the circumstances.

Olivia jumped off her bed and straightened the messy comforter. As she hurried to the door, she almost tripped over a mini dollhouse that was spread out in the middle of the room.

She shook her head. This room was a pigsty, to borrow a term her mother had used often. She couldn't leave it like this. Lucy might get hurt if she crawled in here with all of this stuff lying around. She also knew her mom hadn't been feeling well the past few days. Wouldn't it be nice if her mom didn't have to tell her to clean her room for once? Wouldn't it be nice if her mom walked in later today and saw it all straightened up, bed made, toys put away?

Olivia thought of how hard St. Thérèse had worked in the convent. Surely she could spend some time picking up her room.

"In a minute, Mom! I just want to pick up a little!" she called.

She ended up spending the next half hour straightening up her room. First there was the skirt and blouse she had worn to Mass that morning, which were thrown on top of the bed. She found hangers for those and hung them back up in the closet.

She threw old drawings away, ones that weren't very good. She also tossed out tiny broken toys that had lost their pieces ages ago. When she was finished, her room looked neat and orderly. It was refreshing to see it so clean for once. She smiled as she went downstairs. Won't Mom be happy to see it so neat?

Olivia wondered why, in all of the mess she had cleaned up, she still could not find her St. Thérèse chaplet. She'd crawled under the bed and looked behind her dresser and desk. She'd emptied every drawer and still no luck. Where could it have gone? She could not believe she had been so careless as to have lost it again. She felt terrible.

But there was no time now. Her mom was waiting for her downstairs. She'd just have to look for it later.

Twenty-Four

> *"Take, O Lord, from our hearts all jealousy,*
> *indignation, wrath, and contention, and whatsoever*
> *may hurt charity and lessen brotherly love."*
> *–St. Thérèse*

The phone rang one morning while Olivia was curled up on the couch with a blanket, watching a DVD.

"Olivia! Call for you!" her mother announced, phone in hand.

At that moment Lucy started to fuss, making such a racket that Olivia had to take the phone call in a quieter part of the house.

"Hey, it's me!" said a familiar voice.

"Hayley. Hi," she said tentatively. It was the first time they had spoken since the incident on Halloween night.

"What're you doing?"

Olivia paused, feeling awkward. She had told herself that she was going to give Hayley another chance, but it felt strange somehow. Hayley was acting like nothing had happened on Halloween night, glossing over the incident.

"Watching *Swiss Family Robinson*."

"Oh. Listen, Olivia. About Halloween…"

"Yeah?" Olivia pressed the phone closer to her ear.

"I'm really sorry. It was totally mean. But let's forget about it, okay? You've been ignoring me in school."

Olivia wasn't sure the apology was enough. It didn't sound very sincere. But she took it anyway, eager to be done with the whole mess. It was too weird.

"All right," she relented. "And I'm sorry I told you I hate you. I don't. I just want to forget it ever happened. Chad is a nice person and doesn't deserve to be treated like that, you know?"

"I know," Hayley said. "It was awful, what I did. I want to make it up to you. My mom is taking Sabrina and me to the mall today. Want to come with us? We can get ice cream and walk around."

Olivia hesitated. She wasn't sure if her mom would let her go to the mall with a mother she hadn't met yet. She wasn't even sure she wanted to go with them after all that had happened lately.

Hayley sensed her unease.

"Come on," she urged. "There's a new store that sells hair things and jewelry called Girl Stuff. It looks really cool!"

"I don't know…" For some reason, Olivia felt really tired. All she really wanted to do was to stay home and watch TV.

"Are you still mad?"

"No, it's just…"

Hayley started to get impatient. "Come on, Olivia. I apologized. Isn't that good enough? Let's go to the mall and have fun today."

A couple of hours later, Olivia was in the back seat of Mrs. Stewart's car, sandwiched between Hayley and Sabrina.

"Your mom is so nice, Olivia," said Mrs. Stewart over her shoulder. "And I just love her southern drawl. Yours too."

Olivia smiled. It seemed as if everyone up north made a point of noticing her southern accent. Sometimes she missed being able to talk without people paying attention to the sound her voice made. But it was okay. She supposed she would think the same way about a northerner if she were still living in Texas.

"I think I might start saying 'y'all'" Sabrina said with a determined look on her face. "I like the way it sounds."

Hayley laughed. "If you say so, Sabrina."

Olivia had never met Hayley's mom before. She didn't go to many school functions because she worked some evenings. And Olivia hadn't been invited to her house yet. Mrs. Stewart seemed really nice, though, in spite of Hayley's complaints about her.

They finally found a place to park the car at the shopping center. It was a busy Saturday at the mall. Shoppers had already begun their Christmas shopping and the mall was decorated festively with Christmas trees and lights.

The girls had a good time shopping and walking around with Mrs. Stewart. Olivia loved the new store Girl Stuff. It was fun to see all of the cute hair accessories and funny sunglasses. The entire store was pink, her favorite color, and had a seemingly endless supply of girly, frilly merchandise. She was in girl heaven.

"I love this store!"

"I know, isn't it the best? I heard they do birthday parties," Sabrina remarked. "I'm going to ask my parents if I can have mine here."

"Oh Sabrina," Hayley rolled her eyes in mock aggravation. "Your birthday's not until April!"

"I don't care! I'm going to take one of these anyway," she laughed as she took a birthday party brochure from the counter. "I like to plan things in advance!"

Olivia giggled. She wondered if her parents would ever consider letting her have a birthday party in this fun store. She looked around, taking it all in. Pop music played in the background and colored lights were everywhere. Pink sequined mirrors were lined up along the counters so customers could try on jewelry and funny sunglasses. Further along the counter was a big chair where a girl about her age was sitting, looking anxious.

"Is it going to hurt?" the girl asked over the loud music.

"Real quick and then it will be over," said a teenaged girl in a pink apron holding some sort of tool in her hand.

"Now hold really still, Rachel, Love," said the girl's mom, who stood beside her.

The girl in the pink apron swabbed the girl's left earlobe with a cotton ball dipped in alcohol.

"Ready?" the teenager asked.

"Um…I guess…" the girl closed her eyes, gripped the sides of her chair, and winced in anticipation of the pain she knew was to come.

"One, two, three!" and with that the teenager squeezed the tool around the young girl's earlobe.

"Eieee!" she yelped. She slowly opened her eyes, letting them adjust to the pink strobe lights. She paused, then let out a huge grin.

"Hey," she cried. "That wasn't bad at all! Do the other one!"

The teenaged girl laughed. "See, I told you. It will be a little sore but the pain will die down in a couple hours."

She noticed Olivia watching her intently and stopped.

"Hi there," she said in a chipper voice. "Are you next?"

"Me? Oh, no…I'm just watching," Olivia said, flustered.

"Are you sure? We're running a special today—half off ear piercing for our grand opening!" She eyed Olivia's ears. "Your ears would look totally cute with these silver studs Rachel's getting." She gestured toward the girl in the chair.

"Um, no thanks."

The girl in the apron shrugged her shoulders. "Just think about it. You don't want to miss out on the special. Today's the last day. Tomorrow it will be full price."

Olivia stood and watched until Rachel was done. The girl gave Rachel a fuzzy hand mirror (pink, of course) for her to examine her newly pierced ears.

"They look beautiful," Rachel gushed. "Thanks, Mom!"

At that moment Hayley wandered over. "Watcha doing?"

"Oh, just watching this girl get her ears pierced."

Hayley's hand traveled up to her own pierced ears. "Wow! It would be so fun to get your ears pierced here. Plus, they give you a discount on their earrings if you do!" She looked around. "I'm going to go find the earrings. Maybe I'll get a pair," she said.

"I think I'm getting a little too old for this pink overload," Mrs. Stewart came over and said good-naturedly. "Is it okay if I just wait by the entrance, girls?"

Olivia nodded and noticed a display of fuzzy purple diaries with locks. Alongside them were furry pens in all colors of the rainbow. Fingering them, she couldn't contain her excitement.

Her mom had given her a little spending money that she had tucked into her purse. She also had some allowance in her wallet that she'd been saving. Her only problem was, what to use it on?

Olivia's eye was drawn to a necklace rack with many cute designs. She took a plastic green necklace with a pink butterfly on it off of the rack and slipped it over her head.

She turned to the girls. "What do y'all think?"

"Oooh, I love it!" cried Hayley. "Mind if I get one too?"

"Sure!" Olivia didn't mind. She was secretly glad her choice was good enough for Hayley to like, too. Hayley chose one in another color.

"There, I'll get the blue one so we don't have the same one."

Sabrina grabbed a yellow one off of the necklace rack. "I've got some extra money. How about if I get this one and we all have one?"

Olivia liked that idea. They could look like triplets.

She was having such a fun time, but she couldn't get the lucky girl Rachel out of her mind. She looked over and saw Rachel and her mom picking out cute earrings at the counter. She secretly wished she was her. What fun to have your ears pierced and pick out new earrings. If only her parents would let her…

But that was not likely to happen. Her parents had strict views on ear piercing. She had to be at least thirteen before her parents would even consider it. Even though girls couldn't wear earrings to school because it was against the uniform code, it would still be fun to be able to wear them on weekends and vacations. She hated being one of the only ones without pierced ears. Even Jenna had pierced ears, although she really never talked about it to Olivia.

Olivia sighed heavily. She tried to distract herself by trying on pretty rings. She saw a fun ring that changed colors and was supposed to identify what mood you were in. It came with a chart to explain what the colors meant.

They each took turns trying on the ring to decipher their moods.

"Light green…" Sabrina scanned the chart. "It says I'm feeling mischievous!" She let out a cackle. "Maybe I am!"

"Let me try," said Hayley as she snatched the ring off of Sabrina's finger. Within seconds the ring turned to a shade of white.

"What does white mean?"

Olivia glanced at the card. "Hayley, it says you're angry!"

"But I'm not angry!" she cried, her mouth agape.

"But that's what it says," Olivia teased her good-naturedly.

"But I'm *not!*"

"She is now!" cried Sabrina. Everyone laughed as Hayley turned red and burst into giggles. The three of them were having such a good time. She was so relieved and happy. She knew it meant that her prayers to St. Thérèse were being heard. They were having fun together and there were no problems. Nobody was making fun of Chad or Jenna, or saying anything mean. It was a perfect afternoon. If only...

Rachel and her mom exited the store, the girl holding a small pink bag Olivia supposed was filled with brand-new earrings.

"Thanks, Mom!" Olivia heard her say as they left.

Olivia frowned. She could feel a little bit of jealousy creeping inside of her. She knew it was wrong, but she couldn't help herself. Rachel was so lucky!

"Hayley? Is that you?" the pink-aproned girl cried.

Hayley spun around.

"Jessica, Hi!"

"Omigosh, I thought that was you but I was busy at the ear piercing station. How's Ryan?" she wanted to know.

"He's fine. I think he's working today."

"Oh. Well, tell him I'll see him tonight," the girl said with a twinkle in her eyes and a big smile. "We're going to the movies. And I just saw your mom. Tell her I said hi!"

"Sure, Jessica," Hayley said, then turned so her back faced Jessica. "My brother Ryan's girlfriend," she whispered to Olivia. "She's really cool, but she's a little too ga-ga over him if you ask me. Teenagers!"

The girls paid for their purchases and met Mrs. Stewart by the entrance to the store.

"Was that Jessica inside?" Mrs. Stewart asked. "What a fun job."

Olivia thought so, too. Maybe when she turned sixteen she could get a job working here.

"Who's up for ice cream?"

The girls could not say no to Mrs. Stewart's suggestion. They happily ventured over to the ice cream shop a few doors down from the store.

They sat on a ledge in the middle of the mall, licking their ice cream cones, when a lady Mrs. Stewart knew came up to them.

"Francine? It's been ages!"

The two ladies hugged and started a long conversation.

Olivia looked down at her half-finished ice cream cone. Strangely, her stomach felt too full to finish it.

"Olivia, are you okay?" asked Sabrina.

"Sure, why?"

"I don't know. You look a little sick."

Hayley nodded in agreement.

It made Olivia feel good that her friends noticed she wasn't feeling well. But they were right; she felt like she was coming down with something. Or maybe she was just tired.

"No, I'm fine," she assured them. She didn't want anything to spoil the fun day she was having. If the girls made too big of a deal out of it, Mrs. Stewart might decide it was time to go home, and she didn't want that.

Hayley, now finished with her ice cream, was getting incredibly bored. Sabrina sat on her hands and swung her feet from the ledge. "I'm tired of sitting here," she whispered.

"Mom," Hayley moaned. "Can we go back to Girl Stuff?"

Mrs. Stewart nodded absentmindedly, still engrossed in her conversation with the lady.

Hayley seized the opportunity. "Come on, let's go."

The two girls jumped off the ledge and Olivia, after tossing her ice cream into a trash can, followed them back into the pink lights of Girl Stuff, where they proceeded to look at the same merchandise they had seen earlier.

They wandered over to the pierced earrings.

Sabrina pulled some down and held them up to Olivia's ear. "These would look so cute on you, Olivia!"

Hayley agreed. "And they'd match your new necklace!"

Olivia frowned. "I know that, but y'all know I don't *have* pierced ears."

"Yeah." Hayley sighed. "It's too bad."

"Really too bad," agreed Sabrina. A slow grin began to creep across Sabrina's face. "I've got an idea."

Hayley smiled too. "I think I know what you're thinking."

"You do?"

"Yes, I do." She turned to Olivia. "How much money do you have left?"

Olivia narrowed her eyes. "Why?"

"Because the sign says it's only $15 today. Normally it's $30."

"What difference does it make? You know my parents won't let me."

Hayley chose to ignore this and tugged at Sabrina's purse. "Don't you get it? It's now or never! Open your wallet. How much do you have?"

Sabrina pulled out a crumpled-up five and two ones.

"I've got $5," said Hayley hurriedly. "Olivia, how about you?"

Olivia shook her head. "No way, Hayley. My parents would be so mad. I'd get in a ton of trouble."

"You do want pierced ears, don't you, Olivia?" asked Sabrina.

"Well, yeah, but…"

"Once you have them, they can't say no," Sabrina reasoned.

"Come on, even your geeky friend Jenna has pierced ears, Olivia! All we need is three bucks," Hayley said.

Olivia winced at Hayley's remark.

"Don't say that about Jenna, Hayley," she said quietly.

Suddenly Rachel and her mother came back into the store.

"I'm so glad you came back!" cried Jessica. "You wouldn't want to forget your other bag!"

Rachel's mom smiled. "Oh, don't worry. Rachel would have had us race right back here if we had come home without the second bag!"

Olivia felt a surge of jealousy and anger. Rachel had *another* bag of earrings? This was too much!

She turned to Hayley. "I have three dollars," she said flatly.

"That's enough!" she said. "Come on!"

"Wait!" cried Sabrina in a hushed whisper. "We've got the money, but big deal. They're not going to pierce Olivia's ears without a parent here. My mom had to be with me."

"Oh, that's right," said Hayley with a frown. "Hmmm…Let me work on that." She glanced toward the counter where Jessica was arranging earrings.

"Hey, Jessica," she called sweetly as she walked over. "Do you think you could do me a tiny favor?"

Olivia turned toward Sabrina. "I don't know about this…Is this okay?"

"Of course it is," Sabrina reassured her. "Jessica's a friend of Hayley's family. I'm sure it will be fine."

The next thing Olivia knew, Jessica was waving her over to sit in the big chair.

"I'm really not supposed to do this, girls," Jessica confided, "but since Mrs. Stewart is here with you guys and Ryan's my boyfriend," she said with a dreamy look on her face when she said the word *boyfriend,* "then I guess it's okay. Just don't tell anyone."

Olivia felt sweaty as she sat in the vinyl chair, looking at the pink flashing lights blinking around the store. But she had a sense of excitement, too. She badly wanted pierced ears.

Jessica held a tray of little stud earrings in Olivia's lap. "You get to pick one pair. Which one?"

Olivia studied the pretty earrings in the case. They were so nice, it was hard to pick just one pair. She saw a nice gold pair that were simple and round. "These," she said, and suddenly felt a giant thrill of excitement run through her. She was really doing this!

Suddenly, a pang of guilt hit her heart. It was St. Thérèse trying to speak to her, she just knew it.

Olivia...you know you should not be doing this...Please think about what you are about to do...

She hurriedly brushed the thought away and tried to concentrate on what Jessica was doing. She loved St. Thérèse dearly, but at this moment all she wanted was to have pierced ears like the rest of the girls. She hated herself for caving in to her desires in this way. She felt a little sick. She hated herself for not being able to follow the Little Way right now. Thinking of Thérèse reminded Olivia about losing the chaplet, which made her feel doubly sick.

But on the other hand, where was the rose she'd been praying for? Olivia felt like she had been waiting for a very long time. Not only did she not have any sign of a rose, she also did not have her chaplet! It shamed her to even think it, but she was feeling a little irritated and impatient with St. Thérèse at the moment.

"Great choice," Jessica said when Olivia pointed out the earrings she wanted. She dabbed Olivia's left ear with rubbing alcohol.

Jessica looked at Olivia and smiled, waiting for the go-ahead.

"Ready?"

Olivia glanced at her two friends, who were standing by her chair. They could barely contain their glee. Their eyes were wide and their mouths were open with excitement.

Sabrina elbowed Hayley. "See, I told you I was feeling mischievous!"

Olivia turned to look back at Jessica, who was holding the piercing tool. She swallowed hard.

"I'm ready."

Twenty-Five

"When we yield to discouragement or despair it is usually because we give too much thought to the past and to the future."
—*St. Thérèse*

The ride home from the mall was anti-climatic. Mrs. Stewart had turned on the country music station, which was playing sad songs that made Olivia even more depressed. One of the songs was about betrayal.

"How could you do this to me?" the song wailed. "How could you betray me…"

Olivia closed her eyes and started biting a nail. Those words seemed to be speaking right to her! She couldn't take this song anymore. Her head was staring to hurt, too. She felt a strange sort of headache coming on, and the ice cream she'd had was sitting like a rock in her stomach. She wished Mrs. Stewart would turn the dial to another station.

"I trusted you, you done me wrong…"

Olivia groaned. That could be her parents talking to her, or St. Thérèse, or Jesus.

This was bad. She had made a huge mistake. Probably the biggest mistake of her life. What would her parents think? What would her punishment be? She'd never been this disobedient before. Sure, she'd been lippy a time or two, or even had a temper tantrum from time to time like St. Thérèse did long ago as a child. She knew she'd be grounded; that was a given. But for how long? Would she ever see the light of day again?

She watched the houses and stores go by in a blur through the car window. The gray day did nothing to lift her spirits, especially with dusk settling in. Soon it would be time for all of them to sit down for dinner. Her parents would cheerfully ask how her time at the mall was, if she had fun, what the new store was like. She'd have to sit there and pretend nothing was wrong, that she had not gone against her parents' strict instructions and violated their trust. Her first time ever going to the mall with friends, and she had to ruin it by making such a stupid decision.

Would her parents ever trust her again? Why should they, after what she had done?

They'd find out about her ears, no matter how hard she tried to hide them with her hair. Should she just go straight to them and tell the truth from the very start? Or should she wait? Tomorrow was Dad's birthday. The family had a fun day planned at the bowling alley and then going for Chinese food afterward. She didn't want to ruin Dad's birthday with this terrible news. Maybe she should just keep it a secret for a few days. Right?

Olivia thought about asking St. Thérèse for help, but felt too ashamed. What would St. Thérèse think of her now? All of her efforts to follow her Little Way, and she had ruined it by making such a huge mistake, blatantly, defiantly, even when Thérèse had tried to talk her out of it. She had brazenly gone ahead with her decision anyway. *Would St. Thérèse even want to hear from me after I ignored her?* she wondered silently.

The country station finally decided to air a commercial and Mrs. Stewart mercifully changed the station to the easy listening station, which wasn't much better, but at least nobody was singing about betrayal, sin, and broken hearts.

Hayley and Sabrina, who had been bubbling over with excitement over her newly pierced ears just a half hour ago, were now eagerly discussing a TV show she'd never seen and knew absolutely nothing about. She sat on the end and stared out the window, her earlobes sore, a painful reminder of how she had deliberately gone against her parents' wishes in a moment of self-indulgence. Now it could not be undone.

She glanced at the bags on her lap. One was a Girl Stuff bag filled with the trinkets she'd bought earlier that had brought her so much happiness because it was a bond between her and her two new friends. She noticed Sabrina's and Hayley's bags were haphazardly thrown at their feet and forgotten, Sabrina's shoe firmly planted on hers. She guessed that Sabrina's butterfly necklace was probably broken beneath her foot. She felt saddened to realize that Sabrina probably didn't even care.

The second bag on her lap was a clear bag with a bottle of hydrogen peroxide and a small packet of cotton balls.

"This little goody bag is for you to use to take care of your lobes," Jessica had chirped as the three girls peeled off their dollar bills to pay for the piercing. "Swab the area twice a day with the hydrogen peroxide. And turn the earrings around when you think of it, to help keep the shape of the hole."

Olivia had stared in surprise at the bag of things Jessica had handed to her. She'd had no idea there'd be any aftercare involved with ear piercing.

She took the bag and thanked Jessica. The three girls left the store. Hayley's mom was right where they had left her fifteen minutes ago, still chatting away. Olivia thought of something and stopped dead in her tracks.

"Um, Jessica?" she had called back over the noise of the store's music. "Can I have the box for these earrings so I can take them out now?"

"What? Oh, Honey, you can't do that! Didn't I tell you? You have to keep the earrings in for at least three weeks. Otherwise the holes will close up and they'll get all red and infected."

"O-Oh." Olivia was stunned. She couldn't take the earrings out for three whole weeks? She'd just assumed that once they were pierced and the hole was made, she could take the studs out and put them in whenever she wanted to.

"Don't forget to cleanse them to prevent infection! Bye!"

Hayley and Sabrina looked at Olivia's face, which was ghost-white.

"Olivia, what is wrong? Do you feel okay?"

"Not really." Her face looked sickly white. "Y'all, what am I going to do when I get home? My parents can't see these earrings!"

Sabrina thought about that for a bit, then said, "You've got long hair. Just tuck it in front, like this." She demonstrated for her with her own long blonde hair.

"For three whole weeks?!"

Hayley had laughed. "Come on, Olivia, it's not that big of a deal!"

The Stewarts' car pulled into Olivia's neighborhood. Olivia's stop was first.

Despite her dread at arriving home, she did manage to remember her manners.

"Thank you, Mrs. Stewart," she said softly. "I had fun. Bye y'all."

"Oh sure, Sweetheart. Any time! I'm glad you got some fun things today," she nodded toward Olivia's bags. "What's in that one? Looks like a bottle of some sort."

Before Olivia had a chance to respond, Hayley piped up, "I think it's hand cream, Mom. Bye, Olivia! See you on Monday!"

"Hope you feel better, Olivia!" shouted Sabrina.

Olivia said goodbye and shut the door, but not before she heard Mrs. Stewart yell, "Bye Olivia! Have a great rest of the weekend!"

A great weekend. Sure. This was going to be the worst weekend of her life! She felt very weak and tired. Why was her head pounding so hard?

She was nervous, but she knew what she had to do.

Then she took a deep breath and went inside.

Twenty-Six

*"God gives me courage in proportion to my
sufferings. I feel at this moment I couldn't suffer
any more, but I'm not afraid, since if they increase,
He will increase my courage at the same time."*
—St. Thérèse

Olivia kicked off the covers. It was a chilly night outside, but she felt way too warm to sleep. Her face felt all flushed and her head hurt.

She moaned and rolled over, but instantly felt shivery with goose bumps. She reached over and weakly turned on the lamp on her nightstand and glanced at the clock. It took all her strength to do so. It read 2:20 a.m. She'd been asleep since she got home from the mall, practically. She was all set to tell her parents about her mistake, but when it was time to sit down for dinner, she found she had no appetite at all. Her mother had taken one look at her pale face and had sent her straight to bed, saying she looked under the weather.

Olivia had chalked it up to nerves, but now she found it strange that she had fallen asleep right when her head had hit the pillow last night.

Something wasn't right. She felt really sick—hot and cold at the same time. She wanted her mother.

"Mommmm…" she wailed faintly. She moaned again. She didn't like the way she was feeling; it frightened her.

"Jesus," she prayed softly. "Please help me."

A moment later, the hall light flicked on and her mother padded into her darkened room in her slippers and nightgown. She looked very tired and ran a hand through her tousled hair.

"What is it, sweetie? Are you having a bad dream?" she asked tiredly.

"Mommmm, I'm sick."

Mrs. Thomas immediately snapped out of her sleepy mode and became alert.

At once, she sat by the edge of the bed and held the back of her hand to Olivia's forehead.

"I was afraid of this when I checked on you a while ago. You were okay then, but now you're burning up," she said in a serious tone. "Let me get the thermometer."

A few moments later, she pulled the thermometer out of Olivia's mouth and announced, "102.5. I'll get the medicine."

Olivia's dad sleepily stumbled into the room.

"Everything OK?"

"She's got a high fever, but we can get it down. Why don't you fetch me a wet, tepid washcloth? Not too cold, not too warm."

Her mom and dad took turns sponging her warm head with wet washcloths while waiting for the medicine to bring her fever down. They kept her covered in a lightweight blanket to ward off the chill, which didn't seem like enough, but her mother said that she didn't want to overheat her with too many covers while she was fighting a fever. The whole time, Olivia moaned, shivered, and tossed and turned. The medicine seemed to be taking forever to kick in.

About a half hour later, she started to feel a little bit better and stopped shivering. The fever seemed to be breaking. Olivia's mom wanted to take her temperature again.

"Honey, turn on the big light. It's hard to read the thermometer with this little nightlight," her mom told her dad.

"I…I feel a lot better now," said Olivia.

As Olivia lay there, she looked up into the faces of her concerned parents with the thermometer under her tongue. She settled back into her pillow. The big ceiling light flicked on, illuminating the room too brightly, so she closed her eyes.

"There there, Honey," her mom said as she leaned in closer to feel her forehead. "You just caught a virus. We'll call Dr. Sansone in the—"

Her mother stopped abruptly and Olivia heard her catch her breath. Olivia opened her eyes and saw her mom bite down on her lip. Then she saw her mom glance over at her dad, and the two locked eyes for a brief moment.

"It's Sunday, but we'll page him," her mom continued, composing herself.

Her father, too, seemed a bit unnerved, but kissed her forehead before saying, "I'll go get you some orange juice. You need fluids now."

Olivia, feeling a little bit better and more aware of her surroundings, struggled to understand what was going on. Did she just imagine her mother and father's discomfort, or was she still feverish and maybe having some sort of hallucination?

Her father returned with a small glass of cold juice. She eagerly drank it down, grateful for how good it felt going down her throat.

When she drained her glass, her mother took it from her and gave her a small smile.

"You should be fine until morning. We'll come back and check on you then to see how you're doing. Try to rest."

Her mom and dad kissed her again, but still had strange expressions on their faces.

It was only after her parents had turned off the light and left her room did Olivia realize what had just happened.

They had seen her ears.

Twenty-Seven

*"I realize better than ever before how tender and
merciful Our Lord is; He has sent me this cross
when I am capable of bearing it, whereas before I
should have given way to discouragement."*
—St. Thérèse

Olivia's mom pulled the thermometer out of her daughter's mouth and read the digital numbers.

"It's 98.6," she announced happily. "Looks like the fever broke for good."

Olivia breathed a sigh of relief. Ever since she woke up in the middle of the night last night burning up, she'd been taking the cherry-flavored medicine every four hours that made her gag.

"You need it to bring the fever down," her mother had said, urging her to drink every last drop. She'd squished up her face and downed it as quickly as she could and shuddered after every swallow. She was glad all of that was over with.

"Looks like Dr. Sansone was right; just a one-day thing. Maybe it's going around school," her mom noted.

"Dad? Do we have to postpone your birthday?"

"I'm afraid so, Pumpkin." At her dejected face, he assured her, "That's okay. We'll do it next weekend. You're not up to going bowling and having Chinese food today."

Olivia frowned. Boy, did she ever know how to ruin somebody's birthday. First the pierced ears, now being sick.

"Ready for a little bit of soup for lunch?' her dad wanted to know. "Are you hungry?"

"I think so," Olivia said, looking at her parents for any sign of anger about the discovery she knew they'd made last night. She found none that she could see.

"Well," her dad said after she had eaten a bowl of soup and the color had returned to her face, "now that Lucy is down for her nap, your mother and I would like to have a word with you. We wanted to wait until you were feeling better, and you are. This can't wait."

Olivia followed her parents into the living room and sat down on the beige sofa. This was not good. The beige couch seemed to be where all serious discussions were held, although the Thomas family had not had very many. She could really only remember having two thus far: one to tell her she would be having a baby sister, and the other to tell her that they'd be moving to Michigan. But this discussion seemed heavier somehow; she could tell because her parents looked, well…too mad.

Olivia took a big gulp before she spoke. *St. Thérèse, please help me do this*, she thought. She raised one of her fingers to her mouth to bite a nail.

"Mom and Dad? Before you start I have something to say. Can I just…say it?"

Her dad nodded sternly.

"I know getting my ears pierced was wrong. I can't believe I actually went through with it." Her voice started to crack.

"Olivia Thomas, you knew that your mother and I strictly forbade you to get your ears pierced at this young age. And you deliberately went against our rule. That is absolutely not acceptable in this household, young lady."

Ugh. It didn't happen too often, but whenever the term "young lady" was uttered, it wasn't good. Same with "Olivia Thomas."

"I know, Dad, I know! I am so sorry! It all happened so fast!" she was crying openly now. "I was at the store and the girls were telling me I should do it, and they pressured me into doing it!"

"Olivia, you know better than to follow the crowd like that. We've had talks about peer pressure. Remember?" her mother said, shaking her head.

"But they made me! And they said I was the only one who doesn't have pierced ears!"

"That may be so. Maybe you are the only one who doesn't. But I highly doubt that. Even so, nobody can make you do anything you aren't willing to do yourself, Olivia." Mrs. Thomas shifted on the sofa uncomfortably. It was apparent that her parents did not like having to have this conversation, and disappointment was written all over her mother's face. That was the worst of it: disappointing her parents. It was like disappointing Sister Anne Marie at school; worse than the actual punishment.

"God gave you a conscience and will power, and it is up to you to use those gifts. I realize it's very hard at your age, but you have to learn that you have to stand up for what you know is the right thing to do, even if it means being made fun of," her dad said.

Olivia did feel kind of sheepish. Deep down, she knew that she alone was responsible for her actions, not her friends. She'd been trying to blame her friends when all along, it was her jealousy of Rachel and her own weakness for fitting in that had gotten her into this mess.

"We talked to Hayley's mom and she did not know a thing about this," her mom said sternly. "All of that long hair of yours did a good job hiding it, that's for sure. She felt terrible and apologized for letting you three go back into the store unsupervised. She is also very angry with Jessica for going against store policy and piercing your ears without parental consent."

So, Jessica was in the doghouse, too. Olivia felt bad that her and Hayley's nice mom, who had treated them to ice cream, had to be in the middle of all of this.

"I just can't believe I didn't see your ears last night when you came home," her mother said, shaking her head. "Your hair must have been covering them. Imagine my shock when I saw them in the middle of the night."

"I am not sure I like you hanging around these girls, Olivia," her dad said. "We've heard some stories about how they act at school. Your mom and I think that they might be setting a bad example for you. What do you think?"

Olivia wiped her eyes. "Sometimes they do," she admitted. "But I'm not going to get into trouble anymore, I promise. I think they need to be my friends."

"Why?" her mom wanted to know.

"I just think…" Olivia couldn't find the words. "…that if you give them another chance, they'll behave. And I will, too. And I promise, nothing bad is going to happen."

"How do you know that?"

"I've learned my lesson," she sniffed. "Please don't hate me."

Her dad stood up and sat down next to her. "Olivia, we do not hate you. We happen to love you very much, in fact. But your mom and I want you to understand that you will have to be punished for what you did."

Olivia nodded silently.

"This is a serious thing that you have done, and it calls for a serious punishment: You are grounded for two months. This means no phone calls from friends and no play dates on weekends."

Olivia looked up. "Even Jenna?"

"Yes, of course. No friends means no friends."

Olivia was quiet for a moment, pondering her punishment. She was going to hate not seeing her friends, but at least she'd see them in school.

"Okay, I understand," she said solemnly.

"Good," said her mother, who stood up. "Now, the first thing we are going to do is take out those earrings. Dr. Sansone said it would be fine as long as we kept the area clean. Let's go, young lady."

Olivia stood up and followed her mother into the bathroom. She actually felt a sense of relief that her parents knew now.

"Mom?" she asked as they stepped into the bathroom. "I just want you to know that I was planning on telling you right away, I really was. But then I got sick. Do you believe me?"

Mrs. Thomas looked at Olivia thoughtfully. "I do, Olivia."

She gently took out Olivia's earrings and placed them in the palm of her hand. Olivia winced at the slight pain it caused.

"Do you want to hang on to these?" her mom asked.

"No way," Olivia said seriously. She had no desire to see them for a long, long time.

"Can you just keep them until I turn thirteen?"

Twenty-Eight

"When I am feeling nothing, when I am INCAPABLE of praying, of practicing virtue, then is the moment for seeking opportunities, nothings, which please Jesus more than mastery of the world or even martyrdom suffered with generosity. For example, a smile, a friendly word, when I would want to say nothing, or put on a look of annoyance, etc...."
—*St. Thérèse*

Olivia's punishment seemed to last forever. She had never been grounded for more than a week, so this was all very new to her.

She tried to pray to God and talk to St. Thérèse, but she found it difficult to come up with the right words. Most of the time she started but ended up stopping. Sometimes she'd simply say a Hail Mary or Our Father and leave it at that. It distressed her to realize that she didn't have anything to say to either. She felt ashamed of her actions, and disappointed at the same time that things seemed to be getting worse in her life, not better. No roses were coming, and she began to question if she'd ever get one at all.

Sabrina had called once, forgetting that she wasn't allowed to talk on the phone. Other than that, she heard next to nothing from Hayley and Sabrina. They didn't call, and seemed to stay away from her in school. They never said anything mean, but Olivia did get the sense that they were avoiding her.

Mrs. Wells had switched the classroom seats around, and her desk happened to be way across the classroom from both of them. She wound up sitting in front of Timmy DeMayo, who sneezed all of the time due to indoor allergies and was always wiping his nose on his sleeve, and directly behind Allison Puczynski, who was forever shifting around in her seat and raising her hand, even when she didn't know the answer.

She didn't like Mrs. Wells' new seating arrangement, and some days were worse than others. There were times when one more day of Allison reaching out of her seat and shouting "Oh! Oh!" when she thought she knew the answer but really didn't would get on Olivia's very last nerve. Olivia would clench her teeth and remind herself that following the Little Way did not mean kicking Allison's seat in frustration, even though she did admit that it was an appealing idea.

Although she badly wanted to snap at Timmy DeMayo—a.k.a. The Sneezer—for nearly spraying her on a daily basis, instead she anonymously put a small packet of tissues in his desk when he wasn't looking. She figured it couldn't hurt.

"What happened to your ears?" Chad wanted to know when he first saw her the next Monday morning. "Looks like you poked 'em with a red pen." He made a face.

Olivia was annoyed, even at Chad, who normally didn't irritate her. She badly wanted to make a smart remark back, but stopped herself.

"They'll clear up," was all she said.

Jenna came over to see what all the fuss was about, and gasped when she saw Olivia's ears.

"You got them pierced!" she said, wide-eyed. "I thought you weren't allowed!"

"I'm not."

"Then how—"

Olivia was getting irritated at all of this attention. She mumbled something about making a mistake. Soon, some of the other children drifted over to them, trying to look at Olivia's ears.

"Did you really do it?"

"And your parents said no?"

"Are you in big trouble?"

"How long are you grounded for?"

"That was pretty sneaky!"

Olivia tried to field all of the questions as nicely as she could, but it was difficult. They were all flying at her at once. Luckily, Hayley came to her rescue, and Olivia was grateful.

"Come on, you guys. Leave her alone. It's no big deal. Mrs. Wells is going to start morning prayer, so go to your seats. Go on!"

Olivia gave Hayley a weary smile in gratitude. "Thanks."

"Sure. Sabrina and I feel bad about everything. It's our fault you did it and got into trouble."

"No, it's not. I'm the one who chose to do it. I just want to forget it ever happened."

"You didn't look so great when we dropped you off."

"Yeah, I was coming down with something, but I'm better now. No more fever, at least. Don't worry, my mom says I'm not contagious anymore."

Chad was still lingering by Olivia's desk. "Boy, one more day and you could've stayed home from school. Nice timing, Olivia," he said sarcastically with a smile.

"Chad, go sit—" piped up Hayley, until Olivia stopped her.

"No, he's right. Then I could've delayed giving my speech for one more day. It's really bad. I'm going to look so stupid."

Chad seemed to feel sorry for Olivia. "We'll clap really loud for you." He turned to Hayley. "Won't we, Hayley." It was more of a demand than a question.

Hayley, surprised to have Chad speaking directly to her, responded quietly, "Of course."

Olivia was surprised. It was the first polite conversation between the two that she'd seen. Maybe things were looking up!

Then, when Chad walked away, Hayley whispered to Olivia, "His speech will be worse!"

I guess I spoke too soon, Olivia thought.

"Olivia, you are next," Mrs. Wells said later that morning in her perky voice, motioning for her to come up to the front of the classroom. It struck Olivia that of course Mrs. Wells was in a good mood. *She* wasn't the one who had to give a speech.

Well. Time to get on with it. Olivia collected her stack of notecards and walked slowly to the front of the room. It would be difficult to go after Allison. Her speech had earned a "Well done, Allison! You've obviously done your homework on St. Anthony!" from the teacher. Allison had smiled enormously as she practically skipped to her seat while the class clapped. Her speech was over. She could relax.

All eyes were on Olivia at the podium. Her hands shook nervously, making her notecards move. She looked over at Mrs. Wells, who nodded encouragingly. Chad had a giant grin on his face, which somehow made her even more nervous. Without looking at the rest of the class, she stared down at her notecards. She had to do a good job, it was as simple as that. St. Thérèse was watching, and the speech was all about her.

"My speech is on St. Thérèse, the Little Flower," she began, then stopped. She needed help. Suddenly it occurred to her that it wouldn't hurt to call on her patron saint for a little assistance. Quickly she sent up a silent prayer to Thérèse.

Please help me do a good job. I'm so sorry for what I did.

She cleared her throat and started again, this time with renewed vigor.

"...the Little Flower. She is my favorite saint and helps me a lot. She was born in France..." Olivia began to relate the details of Thérèse's childhood, and talked about how she was very ill as a child for a time, but was cured while she lay in bed with a smile from her Madonna statue. She also told the story of the special moment in Thérèse's young life when she stopped thinking of herself and her childish wants and became an adult one Christmas Eve.

As the speech went on, Olivia grew more and more comfortable. She only stuttered a few times. When she got to the last of her notecards, she spoke the last sentence, which was, "St. Thérèse promised to send a shower of roses to those who need her help."

But suddenly, to Olivia, it didn't seem like that should be the end of her speech. She put the stack of notecards down on the podium and looked out at the class, at Mrs. Wells, at Hayley and Sabrina, and the rest of the kids.

They looked at her expectantly, thinking she was finished since her notecards were put down. For a moment the room was silent. Nobody knew whether to clap or not because Olivia stayed put at the podium. Then she spoke.

"I used to have a really pretty chaplet of hers, but I lost it. It belonged to my great grandma. It makes me really sad that it's gone. It was blessed by a really nice priest a long time ago who also loved St. Thérèse. Maybe Allison is right, that praying to St.

Anthony would help me find it. I've also been waiting for a long time for a rose and it hasn't come yet. But my grandma says I shouldn't give up, that it could take a long time. But I believe St. Thérèse. She's like a sister to me, and I…I know she loves me."

She stepped away from the podium and walked back to her seat. It was so quiet you could hear a pin drop. Then she heard the sound of a slow clap. It was coming from Jenna, then Chad joined in. Before long, the entire class was clapping for her. She blushed and slid into her seat.

"Olivia," Mrs. Wells said, a bit teary eyed but composing herself. "That was simply beautiful."

She glanced over at Hayley and Sabrina, who were clapping too. Hayley looked surprised. It occurred to Olivia that this was one of the very few times Hayley had a serious look on her face and wasn't smiling or joking about something.

"Thanks, Mrs. Wells," Olivia responded, and the tiniest of smiles formed in her heart.

Twenty-Nine

"Even when alone be cheerful, remembering always that you are in the sight of the angels."
—*St. Thérèse*

While Olivia was grounded, it was hard not to be able to talk to her friends on the phone and see them on weekends to play. Hayley came to school one day bragging about having her own e-mail address, and Sabrina and Hayley were now talking about e-mails they had sent to each other and Olivia felt left out. She felt like they were all growing distant from one another as the weeks passed.

Sometimes during seatwork Olivia would look over at Hayley and Sabrina and try to catch their eyes to smile a hello. They'd smile back, nothing more, nothing less, and simply return to what they were doing.

Her lunchtime routine consisted of eating with Jenna, Chad, Alexa, and Zach, which turned out to be fun, but she found herself missing Hayley and Sabrina, too. Even though they had brought her many disappointments since she'd started at St. Michael's in September, she had to admit that she'd also had some fun times with them, too. She thought of the apple orchard and how much fun they'd had there, and remembered a time when they all went to play over at Sabrina's house and ordered pizza and watched a movie.

When she wasn't in school, Olivia spent most of her time at home helping out her mom with Lucy or reading alone in her room. She tried to pray, but kept finding it increasingly hard to. It wasn't just because her chaplet was still mysteriously missing. She seemed dried up somehow, like she couldn't find the words to say to Jesus or St. Thérèse. This was very puzzling to her; she hadn't had problems talking to them until the incident at the mall.

The times when Olivia did pray, it was usually just a few words about how she hated being grounded still, and how badly she felt about disobeying her parents. She prayed for her friends, especially Hayley and Sabrina. But she still felt like she didn't know what to say to God.

Stretched out on her bed and staring at the ceiling one evening at dusk, Olivia put her hands behind her head and thought about Hayley and Sabrina, Chad and Jenna.

She spent a little time reading the book on St. Thérèse that Grandma had given her. Sometimes she just stared at the photographs of Thérèse, imagining laughing or talking to the saint. She loved flipping through the book and finding new quotations. Some seemed to be written just for her. She was very surprised to find out that St. Thérèse was an extremely sensitive child and used to cry all of the time, especially when she got into trouble. Then she'd feel so guilty for disappointing her parents that she'd cry even harder. *I sure can relate to that,* Olivia thought.

Olivia poked around her room for a while, picking up toys here and there, a stray sock, and a hairbrush on the floor. She tried to play with her Pioneer Girl dolls, even dressing one of them up in a Christmas-themed outfit to cheer herself up, but it didn't seem to work. Outside her window it was another dark, December evening. It sure got dark early now. She could smell the meatloaf her mother was baking and it smelled good, perfect for a cold night. Olivia hoped her mother was making mashed potatoes to go with it. Pretty soon Dad's car would appear in the driveway and it would be time to eat dinner. She should go downstairs and set the table.

She put her dolls away as neatly as she could and got up from the floor. When she stood up, she happened to look out her bedroom window, which faced the back yard, and saw a pretty sight. She loved it when people put Christmas lights in their back yards too. It was such a fun surprise to look out the window each December and see newly hung Christmas lights all aglow, especially in a place you didn't expect. In Texas, her old neighbors had decorated a big tree in their back yard, but then they had moved away and the new neighbors didn't take up the tradition. So she was pleasantly surprised to see the tree all lit up in multicolored lights in the neighbors' yard directly behind them.

Then Olivia saw something else that surprised her, and she did a double take. She couldn't believe what she saw: Four large deer, one with big antlers, were milling around Olivia's yard. She couldn't get over the size of them. They were huge, much bigger than any dogs she'd ever seen. Even though it was dark outside, the neighbors' Christmas lights illuminated the deer as they ate grass and slowly walked around like they owned the yard. Olivia had never seen deer before, and certainly not in her own back yard! It looked like a Christmas card.

Grandma had told her stories about seeing deer in her own yard, sometimes even a baby deer. Grandma said they were peaceful, quiet creatures, but you didn't want to get too close to them, either.

Wait 'til I tell Grandma about this, Olivia thought, suddenly excited for the first time in a long while. *She won't believe it!*

Suddenly it hit her: Grandma was exactly what she needed right now. Surely Mom and Dad wouldn't ground her from seeing Grandma!

The deer wandered away into her neighbors' yard. Olivia walked quickly downstairs to tell her mother what she'd seen.

"Time to set the table, Livvy," her mom said as she dumped a steaming bowl of cooked potatoes into a colander. "I'm going to mash these. Your daddy should be home any minute now."

"Mom!'" Olivia exclaimed. "Did you see the deer in our back yard? It was incredible!"

Mrs. Thomas looked over, bemused. "No, the blinds are down. How many were there?"

"Four!" Olivia cried. "And one had huge antlers! They almost looked like reindeer."

"Maybe they're checking out our new house in time for Christmas Eve," her mother said with a twinkle in her eye. "I'm glad to see you're cheering up, Livvy."

Her mom dumped the hot potatoes into the colander in the sink and shook it out. She poured the potatoes back into the warm stockpot and set them on the stove to sit for a moment.

"Mom? Do you think I could go see Grandma tomorrow? It's Saturday."

Her mom came over and gave her a hug.

"I don't see why not. We'll give her a call after dinner."

Olivia heard the garage door go up and hastened to the cupboard to get plates.

"Dad's home!"

Thirty

> *"When I open the Gospels, I breathe the fragrance exalted by the life of Jesus, and I know which way to run."*
> —*St. Thérèse*

*G*randma gave Olivia a bear hug when she greeted her. "You're just in time for lunch!"

Olivia's dad kissed the top of her head. "Bye, Pumpkin. I'll pick you up around four or so."

Olivia waved to her dad and closed the door behind her. She was relieved to be here. Grandma would know how to solve all of her problems; she always did.

"We'll eat in a little while, but let's visit a bit first." Grandma put her arm around Olivia's shoulders and led her into the family room, which was decorated with a miniature crèche, garland, some old-fashioned Santas, and a tabletop Christmas tree with colored lights that blinked. Christmas was in two weeks, and Grandma had pulled out all of her special decorations in honor of finally having her two granddaughters in town to celebrate.

"Isn't it nice we can visit like this whenever we want to now? I'm sorry about all of this mess," she waved her hand in the direction of the coffee table, which was covered in flower and seed catalogs. "I know it's going to be winter soon, but one can always dream about spring, right?"

Olivia sat down and picked up one of the catalogs, which were from this past spring. "Look at all of the pretty flowers. You've circled some."

Grandma sat down beside her. "Yes, that's a new hybrid of peony bush I've been wanting to try. Aren't they beautiful? I've got the perfect spot for them on the west side of the house by the Blessed Mother statue."

"Grandma?"

"Hmm?"

"I've been reading a lot about St. Thérèse. The Little Flower. Maybe next spring I'll plant a rosebush for her."

Grandma smiled warmly. "I'm so glad you've discovered a love for her like I have, Olivia. She is very special."

"I know. I talk to her a lot and I feel like she listens to me. But there's one thing that I kind of don't get, Grandma."

"What's that?"

"Well, for a long time now, I've been waiting for a rose from her. To tell me that everything is going to be all right. See, I've been having some problems at my new school."

"Is it math?" Grandma asked knowingly. She remembered struggling herself in days gone by with the subject, so she could relate to her granddaughter's difficulty in that area.

"No, not really. Dad's good at that and has been helping me with the homework."

Grandma looked down at Olivia's hands and studied her bitten-down fingernails with concern.

"You've been biting your fingernails again. Are you nervous? Don't you like your new teacher?"

"Oh no! Mrs. Wells is really nice. Everyone likes her." She thought of how nice Mrs. Wells had been when she had hugged her after the note-passing incident. Some other teachers might have just sent her back to the classroom after their little talk. Her hug was just the thing she needed at that moment.

Olivia paused, unsure of how to put it. "It's my friends. Two of them are just…not very nice sometimes, and it sort of…makes me not nice, either." Olivia wondered if she was saying it right. "I mean, they seem to have a mean streak, and I've been having one, too. Sometimes they're good friends, and other times, they tease a couple of the kids in our class, kids who I've become friends with, too. Especially Chad."

"I see," said Grandma quietly.

"And I'm ashamed to say that I've sort of…done it too. But I stopped, Grandma. I don't do it anymore."

"Have you apologized to this boy?"

"Oh yes!" said Olivia fervently. "We're friends now. He forgave me."

"Well, I'm glad, Honey. Why don't you just hang around the other friends, then? Why associate yourself with kids who don't do the right thing?"

Olivia thought about that for a moment. "It's because of St. Thérèse," she said finally.

"What do you mean?"

"Well, I got to thinking about that story of Thérèse in the convent, and how she talked to the nun nobody wanted to talk to. How she prayed for the sisters she didn't really like. Hayley and Sabrina are kind of like that. Remember how that crabby nun who treated St. Thérèse really badly changed because of how she smiled at her anyway? She sure didn't act like it on the outside, but I think she needed St. Thérèse's friendship."

Grandma nodded. "Everybody needs friendship and love."

Olivia stopped then, remembering the rest of the story. Even St. Thérèse was human; she had negative feelings from time to time, just like Olivia did. But Thérèse never wanted to give in to them. She would smile and try to change the subject. Whenever she met this nun, she prayed for her, thinking of all of her good qualities. *It must have been hard for Thérèse to find any good qualities in that sister*, Olivia thought. She herself had a hard time thinking of Hayley and Sabrina's good qualities, but she had to admit they did have some. She thought back to the Peabody Center baby blanket drive and how hard Sabrina had worked to collect baby blankets for poor children. And she thought of Hayley and how she had gone out of her way to befriend her, a scared, new student on the first day of school. Then there was the fun time they'd had at the apple orchard. Hayley and Sabrina had some good qualities to them, even though they didn't show them often enough.

"That is one of my absolute favorite stories about Thérèse," Grandma recalled fondly. She continued the story for Olivia.

"The crabby sister could not figure out why young Thérèse was always so pleasant to her. One day, she asked her, 'Sister Thérèse, will you please tell me what attracts you so much to me? You give me such a charming smile whenever we meet.'"

"Thérèse told her that she was smiling because she was happy to see her! Of course, she did not tell her that she was really smiling because every time she had to endure her unpleasant company, it was a chance to practice self-denial for the love of Jesus."

Olivia smiled, thinking of Thérèse doing nice things for that unfriendly sister, making little sacrifices to please Jesus.

Then she took a good, long look at herself. She wasn't exactly a saint. She had done some bad things so far. She felt ashamed of them.

"I want to be like St. Thérèse. Really, I do. So I've just… made up my mind that I should keep hanging around Hayley and Sabrina and keep praying for them."

Grandma smiled, proud of her granddaughter who appeared to be wise beyond her years.

"What a beautiful way of looking at it, Olivia."

"I just think that if I keep praying for them, maybe they'll realize that what they are doing is wrong. I just...don't want to give up on them...or on me."

"Following St. Thérèse's example is a wonderful way to make the world a better place, Olivia. Keep praying for those girls, and for yourself as well. God can work miracles in everybody.

"And I think it's wonderful that you want to really follow Thérèse's Little Way. But you cannot expect to follow the Little Way without some hardship along the way. It is a work in progress. Do not get discouraged with your failures. St. Thérèse wrote, 'I am quite resigned, now, to seeing myself always imperfect, and I even make it my joy.'

"I just love that quote. It helps me to remember to keep trying, but to love yourself along the way. God does not expect perfection, He only wants you to try your best each day. After all, the suffering in her life—the death of her mother, a serious childhood illness, her painful bout with fatal tuberculosis—was the very thing that helped St. Thérèse sustain her Little Way. She wrote in her book, "I am too weak to climb the rough stairway of perfection."

"Grandma, you know so much about St. Thérèse."

"Oh, I've been reading about her for years. She wrote so many beautiful things that it seems there is always something new to find in her writings, like hidden treasures. Every time I read something she wrote, it's like a new gem come to light for me. She never gets old."

"Grandma, do you think my friends will start to love St. Thérèse too?"

Grandma shook her head. "Of course you can talk about Thérèse to them, introduce her to them. But you can't make someone feel a certain way, or have a devotion. Praying for a person is the best thing you can do. A simple but good thing. Let God do the rest."

Olivia put the flower catalog back on the coffee table. She thought of St. Thérèse and how she prayed for so many people, even people she didn't know—priests and nuns in far parts of the world who were missionaries. She never went anywhere after she entered the cloistered convent. But she did the best she could do with what she had: praying for them to keep God's kingdom growing. It was a little thing, but also a very big thing.

"Grandma?"

"Yes, Honey?"

"Did Thérèse ever feel discouraged…about God and Heaven?"

Grandma thought about that for a moment before responding.

"There was a time she most certainly did." At Olivia's look of surprise, Grandma reached over and ruffled the top of her head. "Oh, don't look so surprised. She was human, after all."

"I know, but she was so holy and everything."

"That doesn't mean a thing. Anyone can feel discouraged, and even many of the saints felt that way in their lifetimes. Thérèse had a trial of faith, her 'thickest darkness,' and wondered about the existence of Heaven. She had tuberculosis, which caused her a lot of suffering and worry. But even in the midst of that she knew, deep down, that God loved her and she loved Him with all of her soul. In fact, her very last words on this earth were "Oh! I love Him!…My God, I love You!""

Olivia sighed. "I just feel sometimes that maybe she is not listening. I've prayed for a rose for so long and one hasn't happened yet. I've been making the sacrifices and trying to copy the Little Way, but I've been messing up a lot."

Grandma knew Olivia was referring to her pierced ears. Olivia also knew that Grandma thought her two-month punishment was a little harsh, but grandmas were supposed to think their grandchildren's punishments were too harsh, weren't they?

"You're being way too hard on yourself, Livvy. You are a good girl with a good heart. You know, you kind of remind me of Thérèse sometimes."

Olivia looked up, surprised. She was immensely flattered to be compared to the Little Flower.

"Me, Grandma?"

"A little bit, yes. You are very, very sensitive, like Thérèse was," Grandma said, reflecting. "And you've got yourself a little temper." She winked at her, and Olivia giggled, thinking of the stories she'd read about Thérèse's temper. "And when your mind's made up, it is set in stone! But you're a sweet soul, like she was. And most importantly, you love with all of your heart. That was what Thérèse was all about—love."

Olivia was thrilled to be compared to St. Thérèse. It was the highest compliment.

"And don't let the fact that you haven't seen a rose yet stop you from making your little sacrifices," Grandma assured her with a wag of her finger. "Remember how long it took for me to receive a rose when I was waiting for Grandpa?"

It was silent for a moment while the two thought of Grandpa up in Heaven.

"It takes faith. Slow and steady faith. Faith that God is looking out for you, always loving you. Do you remember what Jesus said about having faith the size of a mustard seed?"

Olivia nodded, remembering hearing it told at Mass many times. It was one of her favorite Gospel readings. One time at the grocery store while looking for nutmeg in the spice aisle, she found an actual bottle of mustard seeds. She held the bottle in her hands and stared, amazed, at all of the tiny seeds and she had been reminded of the parable.

"Isn't that incredible that all it takes is teeny, tiny trust in God?" Grandma put her fingers together to illustrate the smallness of a mustard seed.

"Looking at such a tiny seed would make anyone think it would be impossible for it to grow into the big, strong tree that it does.

"We are like these tiny seeds, aren't we? When we first begin to love Jesus, our love is like that tiny mustard seed. But when we keep on trusting Jesus and following Him, our love grows bigger all of the time. Before you know it, we're as big and strong as the actual mustard tree."

Olivia had never thought of it that way before. She felt so lucky to have a grandma who knew so many things about life.

"Grandma," Olivia asked tentatively, "Do you think Grandpa and St. Thérèse are together in Heaven, praying for us?"

"I don't think it, I *know* it," said Grandma with a quiver in her voice. "I have *faith* that they are."

It was quiet for a few moments. Grandma seemed to be mulling over something in her mind. Olivia waited patiently as she looked out the window at the now-barren trees in her back yard. Winter was definitely on its way. Olivia sure hoped it would snow soon. She had always dreamed of having a white Christmas, and this year it could possibly come true for her.

"And you know something else, Livvy? I think Grandpa would like you and me to make something especially yummy for lunch."

She went to the closet and took out their coats.

"I think it's high time we made Grandpa's special-recipe tuna fish," she announced firmly as she grabbed her purse. "We've waited long enough."

"Really?" Olivia perked up. Grandma was just the best.

"Really," echoed Grandma. "Let's go to the market. We need all of the good stuff Grandpa used to put in it. And don't let me forget the celery!"

Thirty-One

"My strength lies in prayer and sacrifice; they are invincible weapons, and touch hearts more surely than words can do, as I have learned by experience."
—St. Thérèse

The calendar changed over to a new year. Olivia's grounding time was thankfully over, much to her relief. Mrs. Wells introduced parallelograms, and the fifth graders started to prepare for the annual daylong field trip to a local historical museum.

When Valentine's Day came, a huge snowstorm dumped close to a foot of snow on everyone, closing schools for miles around. St. Michael's was closed for two days straight. Even though that meant they'd miss their Valentine's Day party at school, Olivia enjoyed having what Michiganders called "snow days," and ran outside the first moment she could to build a giant snowman. She decorated it with a carrot nose and one of her dad's winter hats. She wanted to use her new scarf, but her mother wouldn't let her. "You're going to need it," she'd said, and dug out an old one of hers for Olivia to use instead.

She took a photo of her creation, who she aptly named Frosty, and sent it to Claire and Emily, along with a funny note she'd written about how Frosty wished he could visit them in Texas.

Olivia's birthday was on the second snow day, which was too

bad because she couldn't bring in the cupcakes she'd planned on making for her birthday treat to share with the class. She ended up making them anyway, and her family, snowed in for the day, celebrated her birthday by playing in the snow and eating cupcakes.

Grandma had given her a thirty-dollar check for a birthday present, along with a note that said she had ordered Olivia a pretty pendant necklace of St. Thérèse that should come in the mail any day now. Her parents gave her another Pioneer Girl doll, a couple of fun sweaters and matching pants, and some books she'd been wanting.

Olivia stayed friends with Hayley and Sabrina, but didn't see them very much. Sabrina always seemed to be coming down with a cold, and Hayley started playing basketball on a local recreation league and had lots of practices and games, which kept her tied up on weekends.

They still got to see each other on recess, though, which was fun because St. Michael's playground had an abundance of snow. They built a giant cave that lasted until a bunch of sixth graders came along one day and demolished it, much to the chagrin of Sabrina, who declared, "Those mean sixth-grade boys are so dumb!"

Olivia managed to change the subject when the girls talked mean about Chad and Jenna. It was tough, though. Standing up to people can sometimes be difficult, but, like Grandma had told her, when you know right from wrong, it makes it harder to stand by when others are being hurt. Grandma kept reminding Olivia, though, to always add prayer to the mix. "Never underestimate the power of prayer," Grandma always said.

This especially came to light when, one day after school, Olivia found a letter waiting for her on the kitchen table. A letter from Grandma!

Olivia giggled. They talked on the phone a lot, now that it

wasn't long distance anymore from Texas. Why would Grandma send her a letter?

She was glad, though. She'd had a long day at school, struggling with math concepts and keeping Hayley and Sabrina's comments at bay.

She flopped on the couch with a bag of pretzels and Grandma's letter. Grandma always used stationery with flowers on it. This one had daisies.

My Dear Livvy:

I found a couple of stories about St. Thérèse in one of my books and I had to share them with you. I didn't want to forget. When you get older like me, your memory can get kind of cloudy.

I got to thinking about our talk just before Christmas. I know it was a long time ago. But I think about it often. With all of this snow, I haven't had a chance to come over as much. How are things going at school now?

Maybe these stories will cheer you up!

The first story tells of how the sisters in the convent used to do the laundry together in a big water basin. One of the sisters kept accidentally splashing Thérèse with the hot, dirty water. She badly wanted to say something, or make a face so the sister would realize what she was doing, but she never did.

The other story goes like this: In the convent at Lisieux, the sisters used to drink cider with their meals. It seems that one day at mealtime, one of the sisters sitting by Thérèse realized that she wasn't drinking hers. So she took it without asking! And you know what? This sister even did it again another time. Thérèse never said a word, even with her notorious temper. Can you imagine? She must have been really thirsty. What a sacrifice that must have been! You and I have the same temperament, Livvy. We probably would have given her a piece of our minds, eh?

But while it's okay to stick up for yourself and others, Thérèse taught us that silent prayer can also change people. Perhaps she prayed for both of these nuns.

I know you are having trouble adjusting with some of the kids at school. This story shows just how hard it is to follow the Little Way. Don't give up, and keep praying!

I love you,

Grandma XOXO

Olivia folded up the letter and put it back into the envelope. Grandma and Olivia did have the same temperament; that's probably what made them so close. She tried to imagine what she would have done if she were Thérèse in that situation, and she decided that Grandma had pretty much hit the nail on the head, unfortunately. But as St. Thérèse had always said, "Confidence is the weapon to fight discouragement." So she had to remain confident, and, like Grandma kept saying, keep on praying.

"Dear God," she began, "Thank you for all of your blessings. Please bless all of my friends in a special way, especially Hayley and Sabrina. They still make mean comments about Chad and Jenna, no matter how much I try. I think I am losing patience with them. Please listen to St. Thérèse when she prays for me. I haven't talked to her in a long time, at least how I really want to. It seems kind of forced lately. Please help me with that, too. Amen."

Thirty-Two

"My God, by how many different ways You lead souls!"
—*St. Thérèse*

t. Michael's School was all abuzz with the news: the Peabody Center had been so impressed by their great efforts in the fall baby blanket drive that they had asked the school to assist them again in a spring drive. They had been hit with a flood of new parents who needed warm blankets for their babies. It was still cold in the spring, and St. Michael's School had been so generous and successful in the fall that the Peabody Center knew they had to ask them again. Sister Anne Marie was more than happy to start up a second blanket drive at school. Sabrina was very excited at the prospect and volunteered immediately.

Olivia wished she knew how to make some of the blankets herself. She thought of asking Claire and Emily to send her one or two now that they knew how to knit, but Emily had confessed in one of her latest letters that all they could make were scarves, and messy ones at that.

She asked Grandma, but Grandma sheepishly replied that she could never get the stitches down, no matter how hard Aunt Rita had tried to teach her. So she gave Olivia a blanket she'd bought at the store for her to donate, which was fluffy and warm.

Olivia and her mother took a trip to the discount store one afternoon to buy a baby blanket and some other necessities, like diapers for Lucy. They wandered over into the baby aisle. Olivia shifted on her feet, growing more and more bored as her mother went through her coupons, trying to find just the right one for the diapers.

"I'm going to go in the next aisle, OK, Mom?" asked Olivia. Maybe there would be something more interesting to look at than diapers! There she saw a bottom shelf with packages of cozy baby blankets, all marked with a red clearance sticker. "Spring clearance!" the sign above the shelf shouted at shoppers. "All baby blankets 50% off."

She reached for a package and slid her hand underneath the opening. These were really thick and warm. An incredible bargain for five dollars, and they came in pretty colors. She thought of all of the babies who could use these, and felt sorry for them. She wished she could buy up every single blanket for the poor babies. She wanted every last baby to have something warm to cuddle with.

She felt a little nudge then, down deep inside. She knew who it was from and smiled.

She still had her birthday money from Grandma at home. The blankets were originally ten dollars, but were marked down to five. With Grandma's money, she could buy all six of these. That was a lot of blankets.

Her mother wheeled a cart full of diapers and baby wipes over to where Olivia was standing, holding baby blankets and lost in thought.

"What did you find?"

"Mom, I have a great idea," she said excitedly. "I'm going to buy all of these blankets for the Peabody Center!"

"Really? How much are they?" her mom wanted to know.

"They're only five dollars each. And I've got Grandma's birthday money at home. Can you buy these for me and I'll pay you back when we get back?"

Her mother frowned. "Honey, that's a lot of money. Besides, Dad and I told you we'd donate some blankets for you to bring in. You don't have to spend your own money."

Olivia was insistent. "But I want to, Mom. These blankets would be perfect. I want the babies to have them, and I want them to be from me."

Her mother's face softened into a smile. "That's very thoughtful and generous of you, Livvy. Are you sure you want to do that? Aren't you saving up for that MP3 player?"

Olivia shook her head. "No, the little babies need these more than I need a dumb old MP3 player," she said firmly.

Olivia loaded all of the blankets into the cart.

"I know better than to argue when you and St. Thérèse have got your minds made up," her mother said.

Olivia smiled as they wheeled to the checkout lane. "How did you know?"

"Oh, I just know," her mom smiled, and winked.

The Saturday finally came, the day when the student volunteers came to school to help package the blankets. Sister Anne Marie had come up with the idea to wrap them in individual gift bags with tissue, so they would look like gifts.

"It will make them much more fun to receive, don't you

think?" she'd said, and the children had agreed. "Think of how good you feel when you receive a pretty present all wrapped up to open. These mothers are just the same."

When Olivia was dropped off at school and entered the gym, she was happy to see the stacks and stacks of blankets and piles of gift bags and tissue on the tables. Parent volunteers were there assigning jobs to the students who filed in for duty. Sister Anne Marie was bustling around the gym, making sure everything was running smoothly. Olivia couldn't wait to get started.

"Hi, Olivia," said Mrs. Stewart, who was holding a clipboard. "I'm glad you could come today, Sweetie."

"Hi, Mrs. Stewart." She was surprised to see Hayley's mom here. From what Hayley said, she always seemed to be at work.

Mrs. Stewart gently guided Olivia to a card table set up with bags and tissue. Hayley was sitting there writing a message in marker onto gift tags.

"Hi," Olivia said. "We get to work together."

"Cool," said Hayley, capping her marker. "Well, this one's done."

"What are you doing?"

"Hayley's in charge of cutting out the gift tags and writing a message on them," her mom explained, checking Hayley's handiwork. "Looks very nice, Hayley. Try to write as neatly as you can."

The tags read, "Blessings to you and your new baby."

"Let's see, everyone has a job...Olivia, would you like to be the one who peels the price tags off of the packages? It wouldn't look very nice to have price tags on the gifts." Mrs. Stewart pulled out a chair for her and walked away to assist the other children filing into the gym.

Olivia sat down and started to peel. Before long, she had removed twenty price tags. Hayley took a stack of cardstock and cut it into squares with scissors.

"This is kinda fun," Olivia said.

"Yeah," agreed Hayley. "I'm glad our school is doing it again."

"Where's Sabrina?"

"She's over there folding the homemade blankets," Hayley said, and pointed to the opposite end of the gym with her scissors.

The two continued to work, but mostly in silence. It was a little awkward; neither of them had spent much time together lately, and there wasn't much to say.

Chad and Jenna showed up, walking in together. Olivia was pleased to see them, and very surprised to see Chad. She wondered who was helping to take care of his grandma, but she dared not ask in front of everyone. Maybe his grandpa didn't have to work today. They checked in at the front table and Mrs. Stewart led them to Olivia and Hayley's table.

"Some more volunteers for you, girls," she said.

"Hi y'all," said Olivia, wiping some of the price stickers away from her workspace so they'd have room to sit down. "I'm glad you got put with us. Have a seat."

Hayley looked up and nodded a brief hello but continued to concentrate on her cutting.

"This is a huge production," said Jenna. "I didn't make it to the last one."

"Sister Anne Marie said it's going to be an annual thing," said Chad.

Hayley's mom assigned jobs to Jenna and Chad. Jenna was in charge of punching holes in the tags and tying them onto the bags with ribbon. Chad's task was to wrap the blankets in tissue and place them into the gift bags.

"Wait, we have to do this systematically," Jenna said when there was too much reaching over the table. "Hayley, I think I should sit by you so we can coordinate the tags. OK?"

"OK," she agreed.

"And Chad, you should sit over here because there's more room for you to stuff the bags."

"Yes, Ma'am!" Chad said with a salute. "You're the drill sergeant!"

"Ha, ha," Jenna said, and poked Chad.

It was quite a sight to see the four of them all working together. Nobody would have known the dynamics that were there, the uncomfortable hard feelings underneath. But they began to work really well together. Hayley and Jenna discussed the tags they were making.

"They're turning out really good," Jenna complimented Hayley after a while. "I like the flower design you're putting on them."

"Really?" Hayley asked as she studied one closely. "I just thought it would be nice to dress them up. The other ones look so plain."

"They do look nice," Jenna said. "Can I try doing one?"

Hayley pushed a few colored markers toward Jenna. "Sure."

Jenna drew a squiggly pink border around one, with a blue flower in the middle.

"That's a good idea," said Hayley, noticing the different colors Jenna had used. "It would be perfect for a girl or boy baby."

Olivia kept peeling stickers off until there were none left to do. Her fingers were all sticky. She looked down at her nails. No more bitten-up nails, she noticed with interest. *A couple of months ago, I never would have been able to peel these stickers off*, she thought.

"Can I decorate some of the tags you didn't do?"

Hayley went through the bottom of the pile of tags and pulled out the ones she hadn't done. "Be my guest."

Hayley picked up the scissors and grabbed another stack of card stock. "I need to cut out some more," she said, and began cutting. In an instant, it happened: the fingers on her other hand slipped and got in the way of her scissors as they came snipping down.

"OWWWWW!" she cried, and dropped the paper and scissors. The tip of her finger was bleeding.

"It hurts! Look what I did!" she wailed. Tears began to well up in her eyes when she noticed the blood dripping down on her newly decorated tags.

Chad was the first one to jump up. Instinctively, he grabbed a wad of the gift tissue and held it to her finger, pressing down to stop the flow of blood. Then he helped her out of her chair and brought her over to one of the volunteer moms.

"Hayley hurt herself," he told one of the moms in an excited voice. "She needs help."

Mrs. Stewart, seeing the commotion, rushed over and helped Hayley to the front office, where the bandages and first aid kit were kept.

Olivia and Jenna watched helplessly as Hayley, crying loudly, walked out of the gym with her mom.

It was odd to see tough Hayley cry.

"I feel bad for her," said Jenna.

"Me, too," said Olivia.

Chad came back to the table with a spray bottle, a little trash can, and some paper towels. He swept up the bloody gift tags into the trash can and sprayed the area with the disinfectant spray, wiping as he went.

Just as Jenna and Olivia were leaving the gym to dispose of the garbage, Hayley came back to the table, a large bandage on her finger.

"Mom says it will be fine," she said with a sniffle. "But it was scary."

Her mom gave her a big hug and a kiss. "I think you're all done for today, Sweetie. Maybe we should get going. You've done a lot of wonderful work here."

Hayley shook her head. "No, Mom, that's okay. I'm fine. The four of us are having fun and I don't want to stop."

"Okay, if you're sure. I'll be right over there," she motioned.

Hayley sat back down and stared at the table.

"Thanks, Chad," she said quietly.

"Don't mention it," he said. "It's no big deal."

"It is a big deal. After all I've done to you."

Chad said nothing and looked away.

"Chad, I'm really sorry I did all those things. Really."

"It's okay, Hayley."

"Are we friends? Do you forgive me?" She held out her hand.

"Are you still gushing blood?" he asked wryly. "Maybe I'll shake your other hand," he teased.

Jenna and Olivia arrived back at the table in time to see Chad and Hayley shake hands.

"Chad! You are awesome!" Jenna said as she sat down.

"Chad O'Toole saves the day," Olivia announced proudly. But I have one question: How did you know to use the gift tissue?"

"I don't know, really. It just came to me. I knew I had to add pressure to stop the blood, and that's all we had. I saw it on TV once."

Hayley laughed, her face all blotchy still from tears. "Just what kind of TV shows do you watch, Chad?"

Chad grinned widely. "The worst kind, the most violent ones with the most blood!"

"He's teasing," Jenna said with a chuckle. "His grandparents don't let him watch—" Jenna clapped a hand to her mouth.

She stopped and the table grew silent.

"It's okay, Jenna," said Chad. "We're all friends here."

He turned to look at Olivia and Hayley.

"I live with my grandparents," he said simply. "My parents died when I was four."

Olivia bit her lip and looked down. "I know, Chad. Jenna told me. I tried to keep your secret."

Hayley's mouth was agape. "I didn't know that," she said. "All this time I've lived down the street from you and I never knew that."

Chad shrugged his shoulders. "I don't mind living with my grandparents. They're really nice. We don't have much money but that's okay."

Hayley looked down, shame-faced. "I know what you mean. My dad died when I was seven and it's hard for my mom to make ends meet. She works two jobs."

"I didn't know your dad died," Chad said sadly. "Looks like we have something in common, eh?"

"Yeah, looks like," Hayley said.

About an hour later, everyone's jobs were done. Volunteer dads had come with SUVs to haul the blankets away to the Peabody

Center. Chad's grandpa came to pick him up and Chad left with a wave.

When everyone had put away their folding chairs and tidied up the gym, Sister Anne Marie stood on the stage and held up her hand, signaling silence.

"I just want to say thank you to each and every one of you who helped here today," she said. "You have no idea how much your generous acts of love will help these families in need. God has certainly blessed our school with kind, helping hearts, and I am so proud of all of you. I know it was a lot of work, and we weren't without some mishaps," she nodded at Hayley with a smile. "But I know the mothers at the center will be so grateful."

Everyone started to clap, and Sister held up her hand again. "I also want to especially thank Sabrina Pearson in the fifth grade. I don't know if you all know this, but she personally made ten of these blankets herself. And I must say, Sabrina, that they are absolutely beautiful. You should be very proud of your fine work." Sister held up one of Sabrina's blankets so everyone could see.

Everyone clapped again and Sabrina beamed.

"I never knew you knew how to knit," Olivia asked Sabrina above the applause.

"Crochet—almost the same thing," she responded and shrugged her shoulders. "It's my favorite hobby." She'd looked down, embarrassed.

"I think that is so great," Olivia had said, and meant it. She was shocked by her friend's immense talent. She examined one of Sabrina's soft yellow blankets and admired the pretty stitches in the shape of a V. "You did a beautiful job, Sabrina. I wish I could crochet. Some friends of mine in Texas are learning to knit. I wouldn't mind learning, too."

Sabrina laughed. "Sure. But you have to learn the difference first. They're not the same. It's okay; I didn't know that at first, either. Crochet uses a hook, and knitting uses two needles. I've never knitted, but I can show you some crochet stitches, enough to make a simple scarf or blanket."

"Yeah," Olivia said, wide-eyed. "I'd love that!"

Hayley had looked over with interest. "I knew you could crochet, Sabrina, but enough to do some of these? That's awesome! When did you find the time?"

Sabrina blushed again. "Oh, here and there. If it helps keep those little babies warm and cozy, it's worth it."

"Sabrina? Think you could teach me too?" asked Hayley cautiously.

"Sure!"

"Maybe we could have a lesson sometime…at my house," Hayley offered. "Jenna, you too."

Jenna smiled cautiously. "Um…that would be great."

Olivia left the school that afternoon with an appreciation for Sabrina and her generous heart.

Thirty-Three

"Nothing is sweeter than love; nothing stronger, nothing higher, nothing more generous, nothing more pleasant, nothing fuller or better in Heaven or earth: for love proceeds from God, and cannot rest but in God, above all things created."
—St. Thérèse

In early April, Olivia's doorbell rang one Sunday after church.

"Livvy!" her mom called from upstairs. "I'm changing Lucy. Can you get the door?"

Olivia opened the door to see Hayley standing on her front porch.

"Hi! What are you doing here?" Then, remembering her manners, Olivia said, "Come on in."

Hayley stepped inside.

"Olivia, I can't stay long because my mom's waiting in the car, but I wanted to talk to you for a sec. Can we go up to your room?"

"Of course," she said. "Is it okay with your mom?"

"Yeah, she knows why I'm here."

The two went upstairs to Olivia's room.

Hayley went over and sat on her bed.

"Your room looks a lot neater than last time," she remarked.

"Well, I've been trying," Olivia replied.

"It was a real pigsty when I was here last."

"I know, Hayley." Olivia rolled her eyes. "So what's up?"

Hayley turned serious. "I have something for you."

She stood up, reached into her coat pocket and pulled something out. She walked over to Olivia and took both of her hands in hers and dropped something in them.

"My chaplet!" Olivia cried. "Where did you find it? Did I leave it at school?"

"I didn't find it. I stole it, Olivia. On Halloween night."

"You stole it? But why?"

Hayley shrugged her shoulders. "I was jealous of you. Of your parents, your pretty house, all of it. I wanted to have something you had. I'm sorry."

Olivia was speechless.

"I am so sorry I took it, Olivia. I didn't mean to make you sad. But when you talked about it being missing in your speech, I just felt terrible."

"Then why didn't you give it right back?" Olivia asked, still too shocked to be angry.

"It's the strangest thing. At first I kept it on my nightstand and didn't even notice it. But after the weeks went on, I'd look at it every night and it just…seemed to make me feel better. I don't even know why. But after a while I just couldn't bear to give it back to you."

Olivia held the chaplet in her hands and stared at it. After all of this time, she couldn't believe she was actually holding it in her hands again.

"I went to the library and found a book on her with a prayer in it. I started to say it every night before bed with your chaplet."

Olivia was stunned. "You did?"

"Yeah. I asked her to help me be good. I know I've been a brat. It really hit me at the blanket drive."

Olivia didn't know how to ask it, so she just plunged ahead.

"Hayley, did you…receive a rose?"

"Yeah! I did. I asked St. Thérèse to let my mom get a raise. I didn't do it for the money, though. I really did it so she could quit her other job to spend more time with me and Ryan."

"And she did?"

"Yeah. I couldn't believe it, but it really happened. Her old manager left and a new one came and promoted her. And guess what? The manager's name is Rose! Can you believe it?"

So Hayley had gotten a rose. Olivia had prayed for so long for one, and Hayley got one instead. Olivia was happy for her friend, but she also felt very sad.

"I've been praying for one for a long time," she said.

"Don't worry. You'll get one," Hayley said.

"How do you know?"

"I just know."

"So that's why your mom was able to be there at the blanket drive to help out," Olivia concluded. "Because she doesn't have that other job anymore."

"Yeah, and we go to the library a lot and shopping and out for ice cream. It's awesome, Olivia!"

"Do you want this chaplet, Hayley?" Olivia asked tentatively.

"No thanks. I have my own; my mom got one for me."

"Well, I'm glad you could borrow mine, then, when you needed it," Olivia said with a smile.

"Thanks, Olivia."

"Hayley, I just…I don't know what to say. I'm really happy for you…"

"Are you mad that I stole your chaplet? You have every right to be."

"No, Hayley, I…I know it sounds weird, but I'm really not at all. I'm just glad that you got to know St. Thérèse." Olivia would never have guessed that by stealing her chaplet, Hayley would become close to her favorite saint.

"You know what this means?" Olivia asked.

"No, what?"

"Well, I read that if you feel yourself attracted to a certain saint, it's because that saint has already been praying for you."

It was a beautiful thought. Olivia thought of how she'd been praying for Hayley, too. Apparently, she hadn't been the only one.

"I should get going, but I wanted to ask you: what do you mean by 'Sister in Heaven'?" Hayley asked after a time.

Olivia looked up. "Where did you see that?"

Hayley picked up Olivia's framed picture of St. Thérèse. "You wrote that on the back."

Olivia took it from Hayley and stared at St. Thérèse's lovely picture.

"She listens to me. I love her like a sister," she said simply.

"Olivia? I think I do, too."

Hayley and Olivia went downstairs and Hayley walked outside on to the front porch.

"Oh, one more thing. My birthday party's in a couple of weeks and you're invited. My mom wouldn't let me have a Girl Stuff party. I think she's still down on that store!

"Anyway," she continued, "We're going bowling instead. Think Chad and Jenna would want to come?"

Olivia grinned. "I think it's a pretty safe bet they would," she said.

Thirty-Four

*"...you will not have time to send me your messages
for Heaven. But I am guessing at them, and then
you will only have to tell me them in a whisper, and
I shall hear you, and I shall carry your messages
faithfully to the Lord, to our Immaculate Mother...
and I shall be near you, holding your hand..."*
—St. Thérèse

It was unusually quiet for a weekend morning in late spring,
which was odd. Normally, the dads in the neighborhood would be
out cutting the grass with their mowers, or making lots of sum-
mertime noise with the buzzing sound of electric edgers. The
boys down the street would be bouncing their basketball against
the concrete—thump, thump, thump; then the ensuing cheers or
jeers, depending if the basketball had made it through the hoop
or not.

But the only thing Olivia heard that morning was the faint
sound of a dog barking down the street who wanted to be let in
and the birds chattering noisily to each other as the wind blew
softly between the branches that secured them to the oak trees in
the back yard. She guessed it was maybe too early for the neighbors to start doing their outdoor chores. Now that she thought

about it, she had gotten up earlier than usual. She didn't know why; she'd felt restless all morning and, after kissing her parents good morning, had felt like heading outside before breakfast to the back yard to enjoy the sunshine and quiet. It wouldn't be long before Lucy got up and started to make her usual noise and the weekend business of the household would begin.

Helicopter seeds from the maple tree were everywhere. The breezes helped them to spin gently to the ground and they made crunching noises under her feet as she walked in the yard. It was a deep yard, full of overgrowth in the back perimeter, a garden long left untended by the previous owners.

The Thomas family hadn't had a chance to get acquainted with it since they'd moved in. It seemed like once they'd finished unpacking, it was too cold to explore the rest of the yard, especially along the back fence. Then winter had set in, leaving a blanket of snow to cover everything in cold, deep white.

Olivia crunched her way toward the back and, to her delight, found steps that led to a circular garden covered in weeds and old perennials. She stood quietly and stared at the plants. *It sure needs cleaning up*, Olivia thought. *Maybe Mom and I could redo this garden, with Grandma's help. It looks like it needs some love.* She didn't know much about gardening, but Grandma sure did, and she vowed to call her later this afternoon to ask her what some of the growth was. It was hard to tell, it was so old and overgrown.

But there were small signs of green growth poking through the old, brown branches of plants from years ago. If she and her mom and Grandma could resurrect it, what a lovely secret garden it would be, just like the one in one of her favorite books, she mused. It did have potential.

"Morning, Olivia," came a cheerful voice from beyond the fence, breaking the silence of the morning. A chipmunk, startled by the voice, scurried away to the safety of the groundcover.

It was Mrs. Muscatello, the neighbor behind them. She'd come over only once, to deliver some banana nut bread the day they'd moved in last year.

"Hi, Mrs…"

"Muscatello," the nice old lady reminded her. "That's okay, my memory isn't the greatest, either. I remembered your name because I had a good friend named Olivia once. A pretty, old-fashioned name. You don't hear it often enough," she smiled.

Olivia smiled back, her embarrassment over forgetting her name vanished due to the old lady's kindness.

"This garden could use some TLC, couldn't it?" asked Mrs. Muscatello, surveying the brownness.

Olivia nodded, her eyes resting on an old wooden trellis at the back of the garden. "Yeah, it looks kind of dead. My grandma would know what to do. She gardens a lot."

"Don't say as I do anymore," said Mrs. Muscatello, resting her wrinkled hands on the chain link fence. "But the previous owners sure loved this garden. They tended to it quite nicely, until the wife fell ill some years back and could no longer come back here. It takes a lot of physical labor to tend to a garden this size," she said sweeping her arm wide. "It's all I can do to take care of a few tomato plants and pots of geraniums nowadays."

Olivia nodded, scanning the size of the garden. It would definitely be too much for someone who had health problems.

"We've never even been back here, any of us," Olivia said with a shrug of her shoulders. "I bet it was pretty at one time."

"Oh yes," Mrs. Muscatello agreed, her eyes wide. "It was quite the showplace at one time. The owners belonged to a garden club and the local garden society would come to take pictures every summer. They were quite proud of it. A shame, it is, that it had to turn out this way. It's been unkempt for years. I doubt anything will bloom from it now. Some of these perennials aren't getting any sunlight at all."

She paused for a moment before looking at Olivia. "But I have a feeling that you, young lady, just might be the one to turn it around. With a little know-how and hard work, that is." She winked.

"Well, I've got to get back inside. Mr. Muscatello and I are going out to breakfast," she said proudly. "Our Saturday-morning tradition. I hope to see you again soon, Miss Olivia."

"Bye, Mrs. Muscatello," Olivia called after her as the old lady slowly walked away. She turned her gaze back to the neglected garden and moved in for a closer peek. The tall trellis looked intriguing, and she wanted to see it up close.

She crunched her way toward the trellis, over many autumns' worth of fallen leaves, twigs, and tangled weeds, all fighting for space along the stone walkway. The chipmunk that had scurried away earlier found a spot on a large rock a safe distance away.

"Don't be afraid, Chippy," she spoke softly to the tiny animal. "I'm not going to bother you. I just want to see where you live so I can make it pretty again."

A gentle breeze blew through her hair as she approached the trellis. As she reached up to tuck the flyaways over her ear, a tiny pink petal fluttered by and landed on the ground. Olivia looked up to see where it had come from, but could not find the source.

Another breeze swept through the unkempt garden, causing her to look nearer to the back, on the trellis. She softly stepped over to it to get a closer look. What had, from a distance, seemed brown and dead had little bits of green growth underneath the dead stalks as they clung to the trellis. She reached out to touch the plant and pull the old leaves away.

What she saw up at the top took her breath away. For there, underneath what was dead, sprung new life—the life of a green, thorny rosebush with fluffy blooms of little pink roses, arching themselves along the trellis toward the patch of sun that found its way into the shady garden.

The wind shifted again, breaking the silence of the garden, this time picking up more petals from the bloomed roses. Slowly, gently, they drifted into the air, finally sprinkling down onto Olivia's hair a shower of petals from roses that had bloomed; they must have been blooming for days. She studied the contrast of their pink, tender petals, beautiful blooms, beneath the brown ugliness of forgotten life.

Olivia blinked back tears as the realization hit her.

She stared up at the yellow stream of sunshine making its way through the trees and growth overhead. A shower of pink rose petals clung to her hair.

She stood there for a moment, unable to speak, but feeling a love so strong that her heart would simply burst. She was not alone. Love was all around her.

"Thank you, St. Thérèse," she whispered.

The End

"I have always wanted to become a saint," Thérèse wrote. *"Unfortunately when I have compared myself with the saints, I have always found that there is the same difference between the saints and me as there is between a mountain whose summit is lost in the clouds and a humble grain of sand trodden underfoot by passers-by. Instead of being discouraged, I told myself: God would not make me wish for something impossible and so, in spite of my littleness, I can aim at being a saint. It is impossible for me to grow bigger, so I put up with myself as I am, with all my countless faults. But I will look for some means of going to Heaven by a little way which is very short and very straight, a little way that is quite new."*

Jenna's Cinnamon Chip Scones

Ingredients:

1 cup sour cream	1 teaspoon baking soda
4 cups all-purpose flour	1 cup white sugar
⅔ cup cinnamon chips	2 teaspoons baking powder
¼ teaspoon cream of tartar	1 teaspoon salt
1 cup butter	1 egg
3 teaspoons cinnamon	

For dusting: sugar   cinnamon

Directions:

1. Preheat oven to 350 degrees.

2. Spray two baking sheets with nonstick cooking spray.

3. Combine sour cream and baking soda in a small bowl.

4. Combine flour, sugar, baking powder, cream of tartar and salt in another bowl.

5. Cut in butter until mixture resembles fine breadcrumbs.

6. Combine egg with sour cream mixture and add cinnamon.

7. Gently stir into flour mixture just until moistened, adding cinnamon chips.

8. IMPORTANT: Knead dough as briefly as possible. Overkneading will result in tough dough.

9. Divide dough into two halves. Place on baking sheet and pat into ¾-inch thickness.

10. Cut each round into 6 wedge-shaped pieces.

11. Move scones so they are not touching (at least 3 inches). Dust with sugar and cinnamon.

12. Bake 15-20 minutes or until golden brown.

"I promise to have you taste after my departure for eternal life the happiness one can find in feeling a friendly soul next to oneself." —St. Thérèse

*N*ancy **Carabio Belanger** has loved to write ever since she was a little girl. She used to write fiction stories in math class when she was supposed to be listening to the teacher, a practice she certainly does not recommend to her readers. She has a great love for St. Thérèse of Lisieux, and can relate to the great saint's sometimes tempestuous and oversensitive personality. She says that Thérèse's Little Way is a reminder to all of us who feel like we can do nothing, that we aren't old enough, smart enough, etc. We can all make little sacrifices to please God.

Like Olivia, Nancy loves to cook and try new recipes. She also enjoys spending time with her family, gardening, and relaxing with a good cookbook. When she is not volunteering at her sons' school, she usually can be found underneath a mountain of laundry or working on the sequel to *Olivia and the Little Way*. A graduate of Michigan State University, she lives with her husband and two sons in Michigan. Visit Nancy on the web at www.littleflowerbook.com or www.nancybelanger.blogspot.com.

*I*llustrator **Sandra Casali LewAllen** is an experienced artist in many types of media. A graduate of Wayne State University in art education, she studied studio art and art history in Perugia, Italy. She is working toward a master's degree in education at Michigan State University.

Sandra and her husband Dave have two children, Nick and Sarah. She currently teaches elementary school art in Troy, Michigan. As time permits, she loves to draw, paint, sculpt, and create freelance art.